The Journal of Jesse Smoke

A Cherokee Boy

By Joseph Bruchac

Scholastic Inc. New York

Tennessee
1837

October 1, 1837

Bear showed himself to me this morning. The river far below was shining in the rising sun as I sat on the slope. I had just gone to the river, washed my hands and face in its waters, and thanked the old Long Person for its blessing.

This is all I can write for this evening. I hear my mother calling me. Napoleyan has gotten out of his stall. He will not run away, but neither will he move. When this happens I am the only one who can convince him to go back into the barn. Mules!

October 2, 1837

Got up before sunrise. Fed animals. Then took two broadsword corn dumplings from the basket Mother left out on the porch last night. Ate them as I walked our line of rail fence after letting out the cows from the barn. The dumplings were delicious, and I wished I had taken more.

No rails broken or knocked loose by Napoleyan. But I see I will have to replace a good many rails before winter. I have already readied one log and got out the maul and the wedges for the splitting. It is my job to do all those things Father and I once did together. It will be the first time I have ever tried rail-splitting by myself.

Tried to give Emily and Ruthie a hand with the scalybarks that my sisters and I gathered from our hickory trees and which Mother dried on the rack beside the fire. When I was a small child, before Emily and Ruthie were born, my mother would let me help her prepare the scalybarks with a flat stone and sieve them in the basket to get rid of the hulls. Now my sisters refuse to allow me to help them. As if I did not know how to do it as well as they do!

Later today, if we are lucky, Mother will make connuche. It is our favorite! We will have it with some of the honey I gathered from the hollow in the big beech tree last week. Just as my father taught me, I used a bundle of leaves to smoke the hollow and continually sang Father's song to the bees. Father said that song was taught to his great-grandfather by the bees. I only took half the honey and was not stung even once, though the bees landed on my face and in my hair and buzzed in a rhythm much like that of my song. I left some white beads as a gift for the bees.

I spoke once with Reverend Samuel Worcester about my remembering our Cherokee stories and our old ways. He agreed that there is no harm in our stories, although he says those in the Bible are more instructive. He holds that many of our ways are admirable. Though he and Reverend Elizur Butler are both white men, I trust their honesty. Even the Feeler, who like the majority of our people will not hear of converting from his pagan ways, has respect for them.

"They do as they speak," the Feeler said when the two missionaries refused to swear allegiance to George and agree to the Removal of our people to the west. Because of that, Reverends Worcester and Butler served one year and four months in a Georgia jail.

When they were released, the Feeler was one of the crowd of Cherokees who met them outside the jail and took their hands and accompanied them on their journey back to the Mission School at Brainerd. That gratified me, since the Feeler is my great-uncle.

That is all I have time to write for now. My taper is about burned down, and I have covered more than the page I had promised myself I would fill. Now that the Mission Schools have been closed down, Reverend Butler says, there is a need for every voice to be heard. I believe that is especially true in this time when even some of our own people have turned against us. I refer here, of course, to the Treaty of New Echota. I will write more tomorrow.

October 3, 1837

This evening, when my two sisters, Emily and Ruthie, were asleep and the house was quiet, I picked up my quill to sharpen it before writing. Then my mother asked me what I was doing.

Sometimes when my mother asks this, it is her way of reminding me that I have more to do. In our Cherokee way, it is the women who are the real heads of our households. Our homes and their contents belong to the women and the children to their mother's clan. At times, when I hear my mother's soft, strong voice, I have but to close my eyes to picture her as the Beloved Woman who sat beside the War Chief and the Peace Chief, those powerful men heeding her wise counsel.

So, I immediately put down my pen. What had I forgotten to do? I had a good stock of split wood in the wood box by the fireplace. I had repaired the loose shingles on our roof and replaced the leather top hinge of our back door. I had cleaned out the barn, placing the rotted straw and manure on our manure pile, which we will use for our spring gardens. I had good luck hunting today, bringing in the same deer I had hoped to encounter the day I met the Bear. That deer now hung outside. Having used it to such good effect today, I felt my grandfather's gun also needed attention before I replaced it over the fireplace, and so I had thoroughly cleaned and polished it.

Then I understood. My journal was on the table in front of me, the ink bottle uncorked, my quill next to it, the knife with which I had been sharpening the nib still in my hand.

I felt foolish. I should have spoken with my mother about my journal. It was she who insisted, after Father was killed, that I must continue to follow the learning of the white man's ways. She wanted me to return to the Mission School, even though it left her as a widow without a son to assist her about the house. My father was murdered three years ago, when I was thirteen. My two sisters, three and five years younger than me, are not as great a help as I am. I said that I should stay and help her. But my mother was as firm as a stone. So I went back to school. I remained there until it was closed this past year. It is to be converted into a fort to hold the troops, both United States Regulars and State Militias, that have begun arriving in our small Cherokee Nation in an ever-increasing flow.

I explained in a rush of words what I was about, that I was trying to make a record of the things happening to us and those we know in these difficult times. I apologized for not telling her first before all others.

She smiled and placed her hands upon mine. "Wado, my son," she said. "Thank you. You honor me."

Then she sat down beside me to listen. I read her all that I had written. When I finished, my mother rose and placed another log onto the fire. "You do well," she said. "But I have one question."

"Ask it," I said, knowing that any question my dear mother might ask would be one I needed to hear.

Mother said it seemed that when I write in this journal I am talking to someone I trust. She said I write as if that person is a good friend.

I agreed with her. I do feel that this journal is my friend.

"If we trust a friend, we give them our names," she said.

My mother was right. So I shall begin again with you, my reader and my friend.

Osiyo! Allow me to introduce myself. The Ani-Kawi, the Deer, is my clan. My mother is known by the name of Sallie Littledeer. My father was known as Twokiller. My two sisters, as mentioned earlier, wish to be called Emily and Ruthie, though their Cherokee names are quite different. I have also been known by more than one name already in my short life of only sixteen winters. My Cherokee name is Gogisgi, which means "Smoke." At the Mission School they gave me the name of Jesse.

Jesse Smoke, I became, and was so recorded in the Mission records. My friends call me Jess, and you may do the same.

October 4, 1837

Started splitting rails for the fence today. Weather unusually hot. Four turkey buzzards circled overhead as I labored behind the barn with the log, which was too stubborn to allow me to split it, spitting out one wedge after another. By the time I was done it was quite dark.

My hands were so stiff from holding the ax, they felt like blocks of wood. My mother rubbed bear grease into my hands and crooned a song I had not heard her sing to me since I was a baby. For some reason my eyes became filled with tears as she sang, but she did not notice. Gradually the feeling returned to my fingers, and I could hold the wooden bowl of bean soup that my sister Ruthie placed in my hands. I will write more tomorrow.

October 5, 1837

Last night, after everyone else went to bed, I sat by the fire for a long time and looked up at the long rifle hanging above the mantel. I had many thoughts, but my hands were too sore to write. My time away at school has made it hard for me to get used to such manual labor again as I must do now. Today my hands no longer are so stiff, and so I will now try to write more about the Bear that I did not shoot and also about that weapon, which belonged first to Old Turkey, my grandfather. It is the gun he was given by the Americans to carry into the Battle of Horseshoe Bend in 1814.

My grandfather, Old Turkey, was one of those who swam the river and assaulted the Red Stick barricade and by God broke through. He was not one of the ones who tallied the enemy dead by cutting off their noses and bringing them in a bag back to the general. Not that he would have shrunk from doing that. But by then he was dead with a Red Stick arrow through the side of his throat.

So it was his gun and not him that came home from the Creek War. It was not much of a trade, but was worth more than Old Hickory's word. Jackson promised to be friends to the Cherokee forever. Then he ran for president on an Indian Removal pledge. His word to the Indians was worth less than a hill of beans.

Old Turkey's son, my own father, carried that gun to hunt with as I do now. My father never fired it at a human being, even though doing so might have saved his life when he was ambushed by that gang of white men.

October 6, 1837

Was surprised today to be given some of the connuche for my breakfast. Mother had saved it for me. She had mixed not only honey but also strawberry preserves into the hickory nut mush. My sisters are quite greedy for it, especially Emily. Her Cherokee name, which she no longer uses since getting her new name at the daily Mission School, is Laughs When She Sees Food.

Did my usual chores, but no further splitting of rails. I shall do that later. Instead, I spent the rest of the morning working on the wood pile. Then, being the tallest one in our home, it was my job in the afternoon to help Mother rearrange the strings of beans and folded-over corn leaves hanging from our rafters. The scorched corn leaves would be used to wrap corn dumplings. Also shifted the planks on which we had spread out the quarter cabbages to dry. Space was needed for the apple slices, which we had on ash splints next to the fire.

Later, by the fire, I read what I wrote earlier. I see I still forgot to say more about that Bear. I was waiting for a deer to come along the trail, but the Bear came instead. The gun was already to my shoulder, and I had but to touch it off to bring down that Bear. I am partial to the meat of the bear. It is only right I should be, for long ago the Bears chose to be food for the Cherokees.

Long ago, the Feeler says, the people had nothing to hunt. They needed food. So one whole clan of our people sacrificed themselves. They said, "We will turn ourselves into Bears. Then you can hunt us, eat our flesh and use our skins for blankets."

Maybe I was thinking of the Feeler's words when that big boar Bear came into sight. It made me think about that sacrifice, and I held my fire. Maybe it was something else. For the Bear stopped and reared up on his hind legs and turned around twice. Next he fell down onto all fours and shuffled toward the direction of the Darkening Land, the west. Then he turned his head to look in my direction. It seemed as if the Bear were beckoning me to follow him or saying to me that I should soon be traveling in that same direction. He bobbed his head up and down and from side to side as bears do when they greet each other. Then he turned back toward the west and began to walk. I watched until he was lost in the trees.

October 7, 1837

Good news today. Everyone is excited. A rider came in to tell everyone that John Ross is on his way. Kooweeskoowee is coming, he shouted, the White Bird will soon talk to the people.

October 8, 1837

There was much excitement about the visit of Chief John Ross. Everyone gathered to listen to him speak from the back of his horse. He did not get down, as he had many more stops to make that day before returning to Washington. Also, because he is so short, he can be better seen by all when mounted.

Chief Ross will be sending a Cherokee delegation to Florida soon. They will try to talk between the U.S. Army and the Seminoles, who are fighting a war to keep from being removed. Our Chief and our Council are worried that the white people will think the Cherokees are like the Seminoles and believe we are warlike and not to be trusted.

The gist of his speech to us was clear and simple. We must not prepare to be removed, despite Commissioner Schermerhorn and the Treaty of New Echota. Despite what the Ridge and the others who betrayed us did, we must not give up. We must cling to our land. We must plant our crops next spring. We also must not resist or fight the whites by force of arms. We must be good neighbors to our white brothers and sisters. It is through the courts, not the gun, that we will resist.

Here are the words with which he ended:

I shall not cease my effort to prevail on the United States government to turn aside from the ruin they would bring upon our native Country; *yes, the ruin — and for what? Have we done any wrong? We are not charged with any. We have a* Country *which others covet. This is the only offense we have yet been charged with.*

He left us with much to talk about.

October 11, 1837

Unable to write the last two days because of so much work about our small farm. Among other things, had to take Napoleyan to John Iron to get shod. We are not like those of our Cherokee Nation who are wealthy and have Negro slaves to assist in their labors. Reverends Worcester and Butler have openly questioned slavery. I agree with their views, but many Cherokees cannot see what is wrong with slavery as long as the slaves are well treated and content.

Noted that our hens are very nervous.

October 12, 1837

Many in our Indian Nation have been to school here and in New England. We have our own written language. I myself even have a small library, and some of the books are written in Cherokee.

I have a pile of Reverend Worcester's tracts here. None of them are as well written as Milton or Shakespeare. However, the passages from the Bible do read beautifully. These books and pamphlets deal with such things as proper behavior and finding the light of Christianity. These are some of their titles:

Ten Commandments, & A Poison Tree & Sin
Irreverence in the House of God, & Pray for them which persecute you
Translations of the Book of Jonah — Naaman & Gehazi, Patient Joe, & Psalms 116
Troublesome Garden, & Parents' neglect of their children
Poor Sarah, Am I a Christian, & the Bible

On one shelf in my room are my morocco-bound Testament, Shakespeare, Milton, and other books of poetry.

My hands have become so calloused and rough from the work I have constantly engaged in since returning to our farm that it is hard for me to hold a book in them. Much as I value the education given me, it was poor preparation for the labor of farming.

October 13, 1837

Counted the chickens this morning. One of them is missing. We can ill afford to lose even a single one. Nothing else of note occurred today.

No farmer worth his salt can survive without an almanac. So I rejoiced when today I received a package from Reverend Worcester. It contained a copy of the almanac prepared by him for 1838. Printed with Cherokee on one page and English on the next, the *Cherokee Almanac* contains:

> The number of months in the year and their names
> The months in each of the seasons
> The number of days in each month
> The names of the days of the week
> The division of days into hours, minutes, and seconds
> The uses of an almanac and the manner of using it
> The visible eclipses in the present year
> Religious matter at the head of each calendar page
> Useful hints on agriculture, domestic economy, industry, etc.

Reverend Worcester plans to publish many more books from the new press he has set up in the west. It is now two years since Reverend Worcester and his family departed from the Cherokee Nation. He left after the

Georgia Guard seized the press that had once published our Nation's newspaper. I think I would enjoy being a writer and publisher of books. But I will not do so if it means I must betray or desert my people, as some have done. I do not mean Reverend Worcester, for he is not Indian but a white man. I mean other Cherokees who have not stood by us as has our Chief John Ross.

October 14, 1837

One of my friends from Creek Path Mission came by and spent two days. His name is John Cloud, but all call him Preacher Tsan. Tsan is Cherokee for John. Preacher Tsan has never learned to speak English. He was a grown man when he came to Creek Path. But he accepted the teachings of the Bible so strongly in his heart that he became a wandering evangelist. He travels through all eight of the Districts of our Republic, spreading the word.

The Bible was translated from Greek into Cherokee soon after Sequoyah gave our Nation the syllabary in 1825. That translation was done by David Brown, whom I never met. He died in one of the influenzas that prevailed at Creek Path from time to time. He died in September of 1829, the year before I arrived at Creek Path.

Miss Delight Sargeant, of Pawlet, Vermont, was my first teacher at Creek Path. Her eyes filled with tears when she spoke of David Brown. She said that he was one of the most educated Indians ever, having gone to Andover to study Greek and Latin and having even devised his own way of writing Cherokee, which was put aside, of course, when Sequoyah come up with his alphabet. Only one other Cherokee, she said, was ever more educated than David Brown. She has now married that man since his first white wife died. She is now Mrs. Elias Boudinot.

Preacher Tsan would laugh if he read what I just wrote. It proves the point he made to me when I read him my first entries in this journal. When I finished, he shook his head and asked who I was writing it for.

It was a good question and it brought me up short. Was I doing it for Reverend Worcester? Was I writing for myself? Or was this for people I had never met?

"Anyone," I said.

That made Tsan smile. He said that "anyone" will not understand my story. He said that I must start at the beginning.

He reached out a hand and put it on my shoulder. He could tell that his words had troubled me. "Tell more stories as you fill your talking leaves. At that you are good."

"Where would I start?" I asked.

"At the beginning," Tsan said.

I will do that tomorrow. Once more it has grown late.

Tomorrow I shall start at the beginning as we Ani-yonega see it. I shall begin with our own Book of Genesis.

October 15, 1837

Our Creation Story

Back in the beginning, the old people tell me, the Earth was not here as it is now. All the beings lived in the sky, and there was water where Earth now is. So Beaver's Grandson, Water Beetle, was sent to dive down to the bottom of that water. Water Beetle came up with mud on his feet. That mud was put on the back of Big Turtle, who floated in the water to hold it up. That mud became the lands of the Earth, all surrounded by water. That mud was too soft and wet for anyone to walk on. So Great Turkey Buzzard came down and flew over the wet land, drying it with his wings. He dried the land, but he also shaped it. When Great Turkey Buzzard's wings came down, they made a valley and when they lifted up, they made mountains. That is how this land was made, all these valleys and mountains, etc., where the Ani-yonega live. We are the original children of that land. We remember what it was like before the Earth was here. We are the ones who live between the Above Land and the Below land.

October 16, 1837

I read my last entry to Tsan. He thinks it's adequate. It shows how we feel that we are part of this land, rightly ours. But he said maybe I should give a short history of how we came to this point where the white people, especially the Georgians, want us to leave. Since he must attend a sacramental meeting at Brainerd, he will not be able to respond to what I shall write. But I will try to get this as right and clear as is possible.

October 17, 1837

Today I spent most of the day drawing in logs. Some are for firewood, and others split for more rail fencing. Being a mule, Napoleyan had other ideas. I spent as much time enticing him to move as I did engaging in any real work. Yet I know that he has a fondness for me. When at last I sat and put my head down in despair, he came over and nuzzled me. From then on he worked twice as hard as a team of horses would work. However, as I put him into the barn this evening, he kicked the side of his stall so hard that he broke one board and dislodged three others.

Tonight I will try to tell another story. I shall relate the history of our dealings with the Yo-ni-ga-we.

Our History with the White Men

Back in the old days our lands included what is now Virginia and Kentucky, North and South Carolina, and Georgia. We lived in villages, some big, some small. Every one of our towns had its own chiefs and its own council. We did not have one chief or a king back then. Sometimes we made war, but mostly we were at peace.

Then the Spanish came through. They were the first of the Yo-ni-ga-we, the strange new people with pale faces. But they continued going and stayed not, leaving behind some dead and even an iron helmet or two of the sort inherited by the Feeler from his great-grandfather.

Next were the Virginia settlers, who stayed. When they attacked our villages, we defeated them and for more than a hundred years the British traded with us. They also built forts. When they took some of our chiefs captive in one of those forts in 1759, it started a war. This time the British were too strong for us. They drove our people into the hills. Some of our chiefs signed a treaty giving up land. But it was not sufficient.

More and more white settlers came in like a flood of water through a broken beaver dam. It was no longer the British, but the United States with whom we had to deal. Some of our leaders took up the hatchet. Tsiyu Gansini or Dragging Canoe and his Chickamauga Cherokees did not give up the struggle, even after Kentucky was sold to white men.

> *We had hoped, Dragging Canoe said, the white men would not be willing to travel beyond the mountains; now that hope is gone. The whole country, which the Cherokees and their fathers so long occupied, will be demanded, and the remnant of the Ani-yonega, once so great and formidable, will be compelled to seek refuge in some distant wilderness. Should we not therefore run all risks, and incur all consequence, rather than submit to further laceration of our country? Such treaties are all right for men who are too old to hunt or fight. As for me, I have my young warriors about me. We will have our land.*

A long and bloody war ensued, ending in 1794 when peace was signed at Tellico Blockhouse. We Cherokees promised to never again make war with the United States. We now had a Principal Chief. We set up a capital for our nation at New Echota, holding on to a small part of our homeland where the new states of Georgia, Tennessee, and North Carolina came together. But the aim of the United States is to move all Indians west of the Great River, the Mississippi. Now, just as Dragging Canoe feared half a century ago, we are told we must all leave our homeland.

Some of our people have given in. They have gone to the Cherokee Agency at Calhoun, Tennessee, where the troops are gathering parties of Cherokees to move them west.

October 18, 1837

It took me all evening to write last night's entry. It was slow going. I felt as if I were pushing a plow without a mule to pull it and only finished one furrow from running into stumps.

Also, in the writing of our history I did not mention the many friends we have had among the white people. Many white men and women have married Cherokees and have thrown their lot in with us. I have before me a newspaper containing the resolution signed by hundreds of good Christians in Philadelphia who condemn the order for our removal to the west. Even General Wool, the soldier sent to oversee our Removal, resigned his post rather than carry on the onerous and unfair duty assigned to him.

Yet, even as I write this, another party of Cherokee émigrés are ready to leave under military escort from the

Cherokee Agency at Calhoun, Tennessee. Too many things are happening. Who can untangle all these twisted threads? It is too much for me. I can write no further. I shall give up this task.

November 3, 1837

The Feeler has seen 110 winters. It is not uncommon for people in our Nation to enjoy a great old age, but he is the oldest man I know. Yet his hair is still thick and black, his eyes are keen, and he still walks as much as twenty miles each day, plants and hoes his own cornfields, and often leads the songs at ball dances, dancing all night about the fire. He has outlived seven wives and fourteen of his children by his own count. Despite his age, he was one of the first in our town to learn Sequoyah's writing. He uses it to record the Sacred Formulas, powerful chants that can bring health or destroy an enemy. This, he feels, is the most worthy use of writing. His distrust of other ways of using it stems from a century of watching white men solemnly write down agreements upon their talking leaves. The Feeler has concluded that the white men take such pains to write down their promises to the Indians to make certain that they will remember to break them all.

Since his own age is almost ten times that of my own, his wisdom is that much greater. We Indians believe that wisdom grows with age. Our old people are the ones who advise us. So I went to my great-uncle for advice. I told him how discouraged I was about my journal.

His response was to ask me to read it to him.

I started to translate my words into Cherokee. He held one hand to his ear as I did so and shook his head.

"What is wrong?" I asked.

He then asked me if I had written my words in Cherokee or in English.

"English," I replied. I am ashamed to say that after my years of schooling I can write easily only in English. If I try to write in our Cherokee syllabary, I move slowly as a measuring worm going up a stick.

"Then read it in English," the Feeler said. "I will not speak that language, but I have learned to understand it."

This surprised me, but anyone who has contact with the Feeler must grow used to surprises. I did as he said.

We both sat without saying anything for a long time after I was done. I held the journal in my hands as the Feeler stared at it. It felt as if it were growing hot, and I thought it would burst into flames. It was probably my own nervousness.

At last he spoke, telling me that what I was doing might become a good thing but that I was using too many words.

I asked, "What can I do?"

Then, again, I waited. When an elder speaks, he often

pauses as does a deer about to enter a clearing. It first looks about and sniffs the air before going further. At such pauses, a white man talks instead of listening. Then the deer turns and goes back into the forest. So I waited and listened.

Finally the Feeler cleared his throat and spoke. "Write more stories into your talking leaves," he said. "Do not worry. There will be plenty of stories for you to tell as the days go on." Then the Feeler sighed deeply. "Too many stories."

As I close this journal for the night I have resolved that I shall try to take his advice and I will keep writing.

November 5, 1837

Saw several bearded and roughly clad white men on the road this morning. They were on the other side of our pasture fence, staring across the field toward our cabin. This worried me. Though we are not wealthy, we are still better off than some of those white men who are neighbors to us just over the state line to the south. There is the belief among some white men that many of the Cherokees now living here, some of them families forced to desert their homes in Georgia or Alabama, have hidden wealth. These white men, who are no more than banditti, believe we have stores of gold that we have taken (against the laws of Georgia) from our own lands.

Made it a point to sit on the front stoop and clean my grandfather's musket in plain view of the white men who stared over our fence at me. They finally drifted away. Though we are in Tennessee and not in Georgia, such men, who often are members of the Georgia Militia, pay little attention to any boundaries. Seeing their hungry faces reminds me how far we have fallen and how far we may yet fall. I fear greatly for our dear Nation.

However, as I sat on our porch writing these words this evening, three members of our Light Horse, the Cherokee mounted police, came galloping by. It is likely they were alerted to the presence of that dangerous band of white men. They are patrolling to see to the safety of our homes and farms. Once, they had the power to drive away whites illegally settled on our lands. Now they only serve as watchmen. I did not recognize them, but one of them waved at me and I waved back. It has lifted my heart for the moment.

November 6, 1837

Today as I survey our little two-room cabin, our small acreage of land, and our few animals, I remember how things were for us three years ago. We had a larger farm, a modest plantation with a small herd of cattle west of New Echota. My father employed people to work the land. We had no slaves. My parents felt that such practices were wrong, even though we Cherokees tend to be kinder to Africans than the white planters are.

But Father feared for us. He had received threats from Georgians who first tried to buy his land for a pittance and then threatened his life. So he moved us here to this smaller farm. Then he went back to get our team of horses and to see about selling off our cattle to a Cherokee neighbor.

A few days after my father went back to see to our plantation, a soldier came to our door. Like many of the white men under General Wool's command, he was a Tennessee Volunteer. Also, like most of Wool's men, he showed not only politeness to our people but even respect and liking. Despite conflicting orders from President Jackson, Wool strove to be fair to white and Indian alike while making matters ready for the emigration of our people. More than once, he had jailed white men or punished them for offenses against Cherokees, even though each such action resulted in angry communications from Old Hickory.

The Tennessee soldier removed his hat and bent his head. Then, in a soft voice, he told my mother it grieved him to have to inform her that her husband had been killed.

My mother listened with her chin raised and her eyes wide open. She did not cry while he was there, though she reached out to take my hand. The soldier related how my father had been murdered in broad daylight by a gang of white men who rode up to our plantation and shot him dead right next to the trellis of white rambling roses he had planted for my mother.

I stood there feeling as if I were drowning in deep water. I could hear anger in the soldier's voice. I remember wondering why I did not feel angry. I felt only emptiness.

The soldier told my mother that there were witnesses. A white woman was being driven by in her rig. She and her driver had seen it all. Because of that, the men who did it were arrested. The courts would not pay attention to an Indian's testimony, but a white woman's was another thing.

The soldier paused. My mother's deep silence touched him more than any tears. I could see the emotion filling his face and choking his voice.

My mother held her hand out to him. "Thank you," she said. "We know that you are men of honor."

Tears filled the man's eyes as he took my mother's hand. "God forgive us all, ma'am."

He turned, climbed back on his horse, and rode away,

his shoulders bowed by a weight he would carry all his life. When the last sound of his horse's hooves on the red dirt road had faded away, my mother began to weep.

The men who killed my father were never tried. The white woman who witnessed the killing was found dead in her own house with her throat cut. The black slave who had been driving her that day vanished, along with her horse and buggy, never to be seen again. Today those same men live in the house that once was ours.

November 8, 1837

Another of our hens was missing today. I fear that a fox has been raiding our hen coop.

News from Washington. John Ross remains in Washington, pleading that our Removal should, at the very least, be delayed another two years. With each delay we hold on to the chance that we may yet remain on what is left of our lands.

However, in Congress, the Georgians now warn that we Cherokees will soon go to war as did the Seminoles. A strong military force must be sent to overpower us, for we have 4,000 warriors ready to take up the scalping knife. This is a bold-faced lie. Every Cherokee who can take up a rifle has sworn to John Ross that we will not resist by force of arms. Our fight shall be in the courts, not upon the field of battle. We could resist and soak the earth of the South with blood, but we know that we would sacrifice our lives and the lives of our families to do this. We do not fear to die, but we have vowed to seek a better way in peace.

November 9, 1837

I received news today of a lighter sort. The ball team of our town has been challenged by the team of the town next to ours. Our elders think a game of ball is a good idea at this time. Stickball is not just a game but also a prayer for good health. I am a member of the team of young men who will play. My friends, especially Bear in the Water, Snake Killer, Crow Caller, and Otter, tease me when I play ball. None of them can read or speak much English. They sometimes call me "Mission Boy."

"Can a Mission Boy still play stickball?" Otter asked.

My friends say that my studies have made my feet soft and my arms weak. Maybe they do this because they know it makes me play harder. Of all the boys on my team, I am almost the fastest runner and I have never been afraid of getting hit with a stick.

"Remember the story of the Bat," I said to them.

Long ago the birds and animals played ball against each other. One little tiny mouse asked the Bear to be on his team. But Bear just laughed at him because the little mouse was so small. So the mouse went to the side of the Birds. They made wings for him out of the skin of an old drum. Thus he became the Bat. In the big ball game between the birds and animals, Bat scored all the goals for the side of the birds. The animals lost because they left him out.

"It is true," Bear in the Water said, "that you are very tiny. Also your eyes have grown weak from reading so many books. Maybe we should call you Bat instead of Mission Boy. Maybe —"

He didn't finish what he was saying because I grabbed him, and we started to wrestle. My other friends jumped in. We rolled around together in the red dirt of our yard while the dogs barked and the chickens scattered in all directions. But we stopped when my mother threw a pail of water over us. We were all laughing, my mother the hardest of all. I realized then how long it had been since I had heard my mother's laughter.

We will have a ball dance tonight. The Feeler will get us ready. We will meet around the fire and go down to the river. He will use the red and black beads to see what will happen. He will bring us good luck. Then we will sing and stomp dance. We will be well prepared for tomorrow's game.

November 10, 1837

Difficult to write. Two fingers broken on my right hand during ball game. A grand game! I scored four goals. I believe our team won, though we lost track of final score. Very good game, indeed. All who played were pleased, though much bloodied. Will write again when fingers hurt less.

November 20, 1837

News has arrived of the emigrant party that set out by water for Indian Territory on March 3 — 466 Cherokees were loaded into eleven flatboats and taken down the Tennessee River. Led by General Nathaniel Smith, their party included Major Ridge and Stand Watie, as well as a number of families tricked into leaving their homes by promising them expense money. Many of them used up their money even before embarking, by drinking and being cheated by white men who lured them into gambling as they waited at Ross's Landing to embark. At every turn in the river, every port, more whiskey was for sale. Whiskey boats even plied the river, ready to sell spirits to any Cherokee on board who yet had money.

The flatboats loaded with drunken Cherokees floated

down to Gunter's Landing in Alabama. There they were hitched to the steamboat *Knoxville* and towed to the head of Muscle Shoals. Then they were loaded into railroad cars, all of them wet and cold. Thence they were taken to Tuscumbia, Alabama, and crowded into two keelboats that went down to the Ohio and Mississippi past Memphis to the Arkansas River. They arrived at last at Fort Coffee, Indian Territory, on March 28. Despite their great discomfort, much sickness, and continual drunkenness, none perished.

The man who related that tale to me is one of those Cherokees. He gave his name as James Smith. He stopped to ask us for only a drink of water, but my mother and sisters insisted that he spend the night. It took him four months to make the long walk back here. Sometimes he was given shelter by sympathetic white families. Other times he hid in a hay pile or a copse of trees through the day to travel by night. James Smith has vowed to never drink again and never again be taken west by any means, whether on land or by water. He ate a great deal of food at the midday meal with us, praised my mother's cooking, and then set out again by early afternoon. He did not say where he was going.

Hearing this sad story of the journey to Indian Territory makes me wonder and worry about the fate of the larger party that left by wagon from Calhoun,

Tennessee, one month ago. Among them are some of my former schoolmates and friends from Mission School.

Fingers hurting greatly now. Will write more tomorrow.

November 24, 1837

The Feeler came by today to look at my broken fingers. He has visited almost every day. He seems eager to hear what I have written. I must confess that his visits do my heart good. I never knew my own grandparents. As you know, my father's father died at the Horseshoe Bend. His wife passed on soon after from a purulent fever. Two years after that, an epidemic of influenza carried off both my mother's parents. So the Feeler has been the only grandfather I have known, sharing with me such things as a grandfather might share with a favored grandchild.

Today, as morning was just breaking and I sat about to mend a horse harness, the Feeler appeared in the door of the barn. He held an ear of Cherokee corn in his hand. He placed it in my injured hand, telling me that I must hold on to it.

Then he turned, motioning for me to follow.

He led me down to the creek and bathed me in its cold waters. As I sat there half-naked and shivering from both cold and excitement, he proceeded to tell me the story of Selu, the Corn. It is a story all Cherokees know well, but hearing it from his ancient voice gave it new meaning. It is one of our most sacred tales, so sacred that in the old days no one could hear the story without first going through a special purification.

First Man Kanati the Hunter and First Woman Selu (whose name is also our name for maize) lived together. Selu would go into their storehouse each day and produce corn from her body. One day, while Kanati was out hunting, their two sons looked into the storehouse. They saw Selu making corn from her body and thought she was a witch.

Selu knew she had been seen. She knew that her sons felt that they must kill her because they believed she was a witch. So she told them to drag her body seven times around on the soft earth. Then corn would grow up and always be there for the people to harvest. But the boys only did so two times, and so there are only two corn harvests each year.

When the Feeler was done with his tale, he simply rose and walked away. I waited for him for some time and finally decided that I should take his lead. I dressed and returned to work. The ear of corn he gave me is here on the table beside me as I write.

It has been a very good day.

November 30, 1837

I find it difficult to write this evening. In part it is because of the pain in my fingers. Napoleyan caught my injured hand between his rump and the stall as I put him into the barn last night.

Fortunately, the Feeler had bound my fingers together with sticks to keep them straight. It protected me from real injury. The sticks have made writing most awkward, but the Feeler has assured me that my fingers are healing well, despite the mule. He has urged me to take a rest from my writing for a time. I shall do as he says after I finish this entry.

Spent much time repairing one side of the pigsty that the blasted mule kicked in. Pigs are the cleverest of the animals about a farm and will find the weak point in any fence and force their way through it. They are especially fond of doing so when it is slaughtering time, seeking to escape into the hills.

Always much to be done around the farm, even a small one such as our own. It is almost two months since our final corn harvest. Our storehouse is full, and many braided strings of corn hang from our rafters. But it will be planting time soon enough. Once again the seeds will enter the earth, and Selu's great gift will return to our people.

January 2, 1838

How have I allowed this much time to pass without writing in my journal? It is now a new year. It is the fatal year when the final deadline for our Removal will be reached.

I have been writing letters and receiving them, yet my journal has sat gathering dust here upon the shelf. At times it has seemed to look at me rather accusingly. "Why are you neglecting me?" it has seemed to say.

I do not know. My fingers healed long ago. Perhaps it is that I am afraid to write because writing makes all that is happening seem too real and too frightening. Terrible things happened to that party of Cherokees who went west by land last October.

In the spring it is said that the army will send more parties of our people west by the water. The soldiers have begun building forts with stockades about them like cattle pens. Even now, I feel there is so much, too much, to put down. My head is spinning. I will try again tomorrow.

January 3, 1838

Those who do not know us may wonder why it is that we Cherokees have been called a "civilized" tribe. I believe, as Reverend Samuel Worcester told me, that civilization is in the spirit of a nation and not in worldly goods. Also, according to the Feeler, we Cherokees were civilized before we ever met a white man. But I think the material possessions of our nation are proof of how hardworking and industrious a people we have been now that we must live in this world by the white man's rules.

So, I will try to wake my sluggish pen by making a list. I have before me my treasured pile of past issues of the *Cherokee Phoenix*, from the very first issue dated 21 February 1828 to the last. Here, from the *Cherokee Phoenix* is a list taken from the 1826 Census of the Cherokee Nation regarding those items associated with civilization that were possessed by our people. To wit:

22,000 Cattle
7,600 Horses
46,000 Swine
2,500 Sheep
762 Looms
2,488 Spinning Wheels
172 Wagons
2,943 Ploughs
10 Sawmills
31 Gristmills
62 Blacksmith Shops

8 Cotton Machines
18 Schools
18 Ferries
A Number of Public Roads

January 5, 1838

Spoke to the Feeler about the bad dreams of drowning that have troubled my sleep. His opinion is that someone jealous of my learning, another Cherokee, has been trying to work a spell against me. The Feeler will now take certain measures to kill the dream. He has shown me the page in his own book that contains the formula he will use. He has also shown me how he has protected his formulas in an ingenious way. Though each page is headed by a title that describes the formula's use, those titles are spurious. Thus a chant designed to drive away a storm may be falsely titled as "To Find a Lost Child." In every case, the true title is on the following page. He has also cleverly mixed up certain of the "ingredients" in his magical recipes. Thus, as he explained carefully to me, when he has written "red," the true color is in fact black, and so on. Thus if his book falls into the wrong hands, it will not avail a rival to use it.

The Feeler has also, as always, given me useful advice. I have been trying to write every day and failing at that aim.

"Only write," he told me, "when your pen wants to speak."

I shall attempt to do that.

January 8, 1838

Enjoyed the untroubled sleep of a baby for the last few nights. Clearly the Feeler's work has succeeded. Unlike a white physician, a Cherokee doctor does not charge money for his good work. It is not considered right to pay money to an Indian healer who has lifted you up. So I gave him the tanned skin of the deer I had shot and mentioned earlier in this journal.

Before he accepted the skin he asked me if I had placed the Ancient Red One upon the trail on my way home.

I was quick to answer yes. Awi Usdi, the Little White Deer, is the undying chief of all the deer. When one of his people is killed by a human, he will pursue them, seeking to give them rheumatism so that their fingers can no longer draw a bow. Only a fire built in the trail will confuse him. To the Cherokees, fire is the Ancient Red One. Fire is not merely the combustion of a flammable substance. It is a being, an ancient Grandfather who helps look out for the Cherokees. Ancient Red One. Red is the color of victory and success.

This is all my pen wishes to write on this day.

January 15, 1838

Preacher Tsan visited with good news. He has such faith and optimism that he is like the return of the sun. Tsan delivered the several newspapers I asked him to obtain for me as well as some letters from my Cherokee Mission School friends. Of course, it is not only through articles and letters that I remain informed. News travels through our Cherokee Nation by word of mouth almost as swiftly as smoke rising from a fire. Here is the news Tsan brought to me.

The new president, Martin Van Buren, has an inclination to favor the Cherokees. He is not filled with that same animosity that has always characterized the Devil. "The Devil" is how Preacher Tsan and many others refer to Andrew Jackson. The Devil's horns have now been polled. His term as president has ended, and he has retired to his home in Tennessee, the Hermitage. Perhaps Van Buren will not show such fear of the southern states. Jackson took seriously Georgia's threats to secede from the Union if her demands regarding our removal were not met.

But it was not just to preserve the Union that Jackson pursued our destruction. Some part of Jackson's unfavorable attitude toward us was likely because of our great Chief John Ross.

Though he is short in stature, Tsan Usdi has never feared that tall grim old Indian fighter. Indeed, John Ross has been David to Jackson's Goliath, defeating him again and again and allowing us to remain while all the other tribes have been harried from their lands like flocks of sheep.

Moreover, Tsan told me, John Ross has made friends with the man most likely to be the new military commander to replace General Wool. He is General Winfield Scott, "Old Fuss and Feathers" himself, late of the Seminole Campaign. Chief John Ross, it seems, has earned Scott's respect.

Our great chief still urges us to hold firm, despite the fact that such men as the Ridges have sold their property and moved, taking their black slaves with them, to the best of the land in the Indian Territory where they have set up palatial homes and plantations rivaling their former holdings.

"We must remain," John Ross said to us, "unanimous in sentiment and action. We are not like the Ridges, who, as you may remember, went through four entire revolutions in their politics within as many months, varying as often as the moon, without the excuse of lunacy for their changes."

His words resulted in a laughter that gradually increased as those of us who understood English translated his remarks into Cherokee for the benefit of the larger number who did not. Though his words were not spoken in Cherokee, he used them as did our old people. One of the reasons why speaking is so important to our people is that it may be used as a form of punishment, shaming wrongdoers.

January 16, 1838

A cold, clear day. Preacher Tsan slept in our barn and departed this morning to continue his rounds. For breakfast we had flat corn dumplings that my mother had placed out overnight so that they would freeze. I believe that there is a special taste to frozen corn dumplings that is like no other. Tsan agreed with me, for he ate twice as many dumplings as I did, which appeared to please my mother and my sisters greatly. Tsan is quite the favorite with my sisters. He, in turn, is always teasing them and brings them small presents such as the blue hair ribbons he gave them on this visit.

After breakfast Tsan and I talked more about Kooweeskoowee. Kooweeskoowee, "the Powerful White Bird," is our great chief's Cherokee name. It is by that name that Tsan always refers to him. I myself often think of our chief by his other Cherokee name of Tsan Usdi, "Little John."

Tsan reminded me of the story about John Ross's return from Washington, where he had been pleading our case in the spring of 1835. While our chief was away, the Georgia Guard took possession of our chief's plantation, evicting his wife and children. Chief Ross now lives near Red Clay in a small two-room cabin made from logs.

Somehow, that story of loss became one of triumph as Preacher Tsan remembered it. It was proof yet again of Tsan Usdi's undying devotion to our Nation. We sat then for a time without speaking, sharing our pride in the honor of John Ross.

February 1, 1838

I have finally received a letter from one of my friends and schoolmates who was part of the wagon train of Cherokees that left for the western lands last October. My friend, Mary Timberlake, now in the western lands, has given me the good news that all of my other mates survived that awful trek. However, she has urged me, above all, to remain here.

Soon after leaving Calhoun, Tennessee, trouble began. People became sick from drinking stagnant water and eating sour grapes by the roadside. So many were ill that the caravan halted more than a week. People began to die, especially children and the old. Among the many buried by the roadside was old Chief Dreadful Waters, one of the signers of the Treaty of 1817, which promised us our lands forever.

Mary obtained a list of the illnesses suffered by our people from Dr. Lillybridge, the physician accompanying those poor emigrants. Colds, influenza, sore throats, coughs, pleurisy, measles, diarrhea, bowel complaints, fevers, toothaches, wounds from accidents and fighting. Whiskey drinking was the cause of all the fights and many of the accidents.

When they finally arrived at Fort Gibson, the land on which they were to settle had already been given to Creek Indians arrived two years before. There is still trouble with Osage Indians who harry and raid the new settlers.

"Unlike our own travails," Mary wrote me, "the John Ridge and Elias Boudinot families traveled the trail ahead of us in fine carriages. They arrived in good health and excellent spirits, after having paid a courtesy call on General Jackson at his Hermitage home. They are ensconced in most lordly fashion upon the best land in the Territory, feted and favored by the commander at Fort Gibson."

The name of that man I once admired — when he used his pen in the service of our people — is there in that letter written by my dear friend. It seems that he and the others who betrayed our Cherokee Nation by signing the treaty of Removal are being rewarded for their treachery. I do not wish to ever write his name again, so I shall refer to him, if the need arises again, as E. B.

February 14, 1838

Finally caught the Fox that was raiding the hens. Used a snare to do so, set beside the loose board where he made his entrance. Apologized to his spirit for the necessity of taking his life and promised I would treat his skin with respect and return his bones to the forest.

It was the animals who sent diseases to our people long ago when we treated them with disdain, hunting them almost to extinction. So my mother explained to me when I was young, reminding me that the plants then offered themselves as medicine to cure those ills. However, respect for the animals we hunt is both prudent and wise.

Snaring and strangling was rather an ignoble fate for the Fox. I would have preferred to shoot him, but could not do so. I no longer have my grandfather's gun. The military authorities have begun, with more vigor than before, to collect all Cherokee weapons. I wrapped the gun tightly in deerskin, which will protect it from rot and rust, then went deep into the hills to a certain hollow tree in a place I know. The gun remains there. I shall retrieve it when a better day dawns for our people.

March 3, 1838

Dry weather continues. No rain has fallen.

We are going ahead with our usual chores at the end of the winter, getting ready to plant our corn. We trust that John Ross will again win a postponement of the Removal. We try to live our lives in an everyday fashion. But we are worried. Only the very young, like my little sisters, seem unaware of what it all means. They are excited by the comings and goings of so many men in uniform on horseback and afoot. Ruthie has taken to counting the soldiers as they pass by. Her count reached 507 on this day alone. More and more troops are continuing to arrive.

The forts have grown in number. We are quite surrounded, like hostages in our own land. At the end of each day I see how my mother stands, her eyes on the setting sun. That direction, the direction of the Darkening Land, is the way the whites wish us to go. It is also, in our old beliefs, the direction of death.

March 5, 1838

The Feeler visited me again last night. I was by myself, sitting on the porch, looking at the new moon. One moment I was alone, and the next he was there beside me.

"Wahuhu," the Feeler whispered, drawing my attention to the distant call of a screech owl. "He warns us that the enemies are close."

I nodded my agreement.

The Feeler then looked up at the new moon. I looked with him. In our old beliefs, Sun and Moon are beloved grandparents. They were given the charge to look after human beings after Galoneda, the Supreme Power, made the world. I tried to remember the way the old people say we should speak to the moon at this time. But I could not. As if reading my mind, the Feeler spoke for both of us.

"Edudu," he said to the new moon, "Maternal Grandfather, we greet you. When it will be like this again, still we will be seeing each other."

March 6, 1838

Still no rain.

Chief Hildebrand has left for Washington. He carried with him the petition protesting Removal and the fraudulent Treaty of New Echota. It has been signed by more than 15,000 Cherokees. The petition will be given to John Ross and presented to Congress.

Spent some time after working in the cornfield playing sticks with Bear in the Water, Crow Caller, and Snake Killer. Otter is not well and could not join us. Began coughing hard two days ago and could not get up from his bed today when we went by and called him out to join us. His mother is worried.

Did well in sticks. Almost every time I threw the four sticks up into the air, they fell in my favor with the rounded sides up. We played for buttons, and I won them all. The others teased me, saying I only won because the Feeler has given me special good luck medicine. My happiness at playing well and their teasing were all half hearted. We kept thinking of Otter, missing his jokes and his laughter.

We Cherokees have seen this sickness before. Some of the many soldiers who have arrived here were coughing in a similar way. Though this sickness makes white men ill, they usually recover. But when our people get this coughing sickness, they often die. Our old medicines do not work against it. Even the white doctors have a hard time curing us.

I am very worried about Otter. Before I went off to the Mission School, he was my closest friend. I have always called him brother.

March 8, 1838

Last night I heard the owl calling again in the nearby woods. Its call was from the direction of the Darkening

Land. This morning the news came, brought to our house by Snake Killer. My friend and brother Otter died last night.

April 18, 1838

Have not written since Otter's death. I say to myself that it is because I am too busy with the spring planting and work about the farm. But I also know that my heart is sick from the loss of my friend and the terrible feeling that ever more losses lie ahead.

It seems as if every other length of our fences must be replaced, and I am still splitting rails. Though I have grown better at the job, it is still tedious work, made more difficult by the dryness. Due to the conditions of drought, there is much dust and the crops have grown slowly.

I opened this journal many times, but was unable to think of anything to say. Now, however, I must write. The new military commander has been appointed. Just as Chief John Ross expected, it is General Scott. Our chief is meeting with him now in Washington, but General Scott will soon arrive to take charge of his troops here.

It seems as if the soldiers are everywhere now. Perhaps there are 10,000 of them. They have built more stockades with walls sixteen feet high. Our people watch as they build them, knowing those grim walls are meant not to protect the troops but to pen us in like cattle.

April 19, 1838

Received a packet of northern newspapers sent me today by Reverend Worcester — *The Boston Patriot, The Liberator,* and the New York *Commercial Advertiser*. One contained another of John Howard Payne's letters in support of our people. For more than three years he has tried to help our people, even being jailed by the Georgia Guard on one occasion. He is now with John Ross in Washington, both of them meeting with Joel R. Poinsett, the new secretary of war. Their aim, I am told by Reverend Worcester in his accompanying letter, is to convince the secretary of war that any roundup of our people should not be done until the autumn so that we may at least bring in our harvest.

April 20, 1838

About John Payne

Met Mr. Payne two years ago. A true gentleman with a broad, intelligent forehead, a sensitive smile, and eyes that are both bright and mild. Also has a fine voice, as one might expect of a composer. I told him that I admired his song and had learned the playing of it while at the Mission School. His response was modest, saying that he had but dashed it off, never expecting it to be so greatly popular.

Mr. Payne told me that though the world has sung his song and nearly every heart is familiar with the melody, he had been a wanderer from his boyhood. He then laughed and told me how when he and Chief Ross were jailed by the Georgia Guard to keep them from going to the meeting where the Treaty of New Echota was signed, the sheriff began humming his song. Mr. Payne then said to the jailer, from behind the iron bars, that he had written that song. His hope was to strike up a conversation and perhaps stir enough fellow feeling to lead to their release.

Mr. Payne then shook his head ruefully. "The man's response," he said, "was a rough oath, followed by another chorus."

"It is the best song I have ever heard," I told Mr. Payne. "It touches the very heart of what we Cherokee feel."

Here are its words:

Mid pleasures and palaces though we
may roam,
Be it ever so humble there's no place like home!
A charm from the skies seems to hallow us there,
Which, seek through the world, is ne'er met
with elsewhere:
Home! Home! sweet, sweet Home!
There's no place like Home!
There's no place like Home.

April 22, 1838

Preacher Tsan visited yesterday. Helped me split rails all day. In the evening we sat on the porch and talked quietly while my mother was at her spinning wheel and my sisters were helping her. The pleasant sound of the spinning wheel can be heard from nearly all Cherokee homes, whether humble cabins or grand mansions — both of which exist in good number among our people.

Long ago, we did not have cloth for our garments but dressed in deerskins. It would take the skin of four deer to clothe one man. We welcomed the cloth brought by the white traders. It was much easier to make clothing. We even adopted the style of wearing cloth about our head in a turban, as did the Creeks and other southern Indians. It makes us rather resemble Hindoos than the western tribes with their feathered headgear. Or at least that is what John Howard Payne, who has traveled to far lands, has assured me. With the spinning wheel, we could make our own cloth and not rely only upon the white traders. In so many ways we Cherokees have become the very model of Thomas Jefferson's perfect American: gentlemen farmers, self-sufficient upon our own land.

Although John Ross still hopes that the government of the United States will give us justice, Preacher Tsan no longer believes this will happen, saying that money, not justice, rules in Washington; that the Senate ratified the lying Treaty of New Echota was proof of it.

I reminded him that it was by only a single vote and that many of the senators had taken up our cause. But Tsan would not be moved from his argument. One vote or one hundred, it mattered not. Just as it did not matter that only twenty of our people signed that treaty or that none of them were empowered by our Nation to do so. Paper — whether it is money or lying treaties — means more to Washington than human lives.

My anger showed itself in my actions. I stabbed my knife deeply into the wood plank before me.

Tsan placed his hand gently upon my arm to calm me. I understood. We Cherokees had given our solemn word. Even though we might feel angry and betrayed, we would never again take up the hatchet. Our actions would prove to the world that we were not savages.

But who now are the savages? I thought. Who, indeed?

April 26, 1838

General Scott is on the move. He will arrive soon and set up his headquarters at New Echota, our former capital.

April 29, 1838

Still very dry weather. The water in the creeks and rivers is as low as it would usually be in late summer. Fortunately, neither our spring nor our well have gone dry.

Spent my free time reading the poems of John Milton today. For some reason I was drawn to *Paradise Lost*. As soon as I began to read, I found myself lost in its grand lines. Time flew by as I read, and when I lifted my head from its pages, the entire afternoon had passed.

On reflection, I cannot help but picture the serpent who deceives the good, innocent Adam and his wife as Old Hickory, President Andrew Jackson himself. Who, among us, were the ones to accept that fatal apple? Will the angel with his fiery sword soon appear to drive us out of Eden?

May 12, 1838

The worst has happened. Scott has issued an order for our immediate Removal. All must hasten to prepare for emigration and come forward so that we may be transported. His address, dated May 10, has been posted widely throughout the Cherokee Nation.

May 15, 1838

A few of our people are following the orders of General Scott. Carrying what possessions they can, they are making their way to one of the three collection points. They are along the rivers at Gunter's Landing, Ross's Landing, and Cherokee Agency. Although the waters are low in the Tennessee, they plan to take us west on flatboats.

Many of my people, like my mother, have made no preparations for leaving.

"We shall trust in Kooweeskoowee," my mother says. "John Ross has a plan."

Our second chief, George Lowrey, has remained here in our Cherokee Nation while John Ross fights for us in Washington. Whenever he speaks, he echoes my mother's words. He also reminded us of the words spoken in council by the old warrior Woman Killer, who died not long after speaking these words that many of us know by heart.

"My companions," Woman Killer said, "men of renown, in council, who now sleep in the dust, spoke the same language and I now stand on the verge of the grave to bear witness to their love of country. My sun of existence is fast approaching to its setting, and my aged bones will soon be laid in the bosom of this earth we have received from our fathers, who had it from the Great Being above.

When I sleep in forgetfulness, I hope my bones will not be deserted by you."

Chief Lowrey has assured us that John Ross is still negotiating and having some success. The secretary of war himself has promised that there will be no forcible roundup of our people before the fall, when it is more practical to travel.

The great majority of our people speak no English, have no great plantations, and live closer to our old ways. They have little or no knowledge of all that is happening. All they have is their deep love for this land and their trust that our leaders, especially Tsan Usdi, will abide by the will of our people.

I observed this today when I spoke to a friend of mine. His name is Standing Turkey. His family numbers ten and they farm land along the Hiwassee River. He and three others in the family are readers of Cherokee. He and his brother are mechanics, and the four women in their family are weavers. Though their place is small, it has fine soil, good water, a small herd of cattle. It is much coveted by the white men who have been surveying it with hungry eyes.

Standing Turkey was on his way to the blacksmith to have a tool mended. He greeted me as we passed on the road. I turned and followed him. Neither of us spoke for half a mile or so as we walked together.

"You are still filling your book with words?" he said to me at last, motioning with his chin at the journal under my arm.

I nodded. It seems that everyone knows of my journal now. I have been teased about it often. Such gentle teasing, though, means that people approve of what I am doing.

The sound of galloping hooves approaching came from around the bend. We stepped to the side, climbing over a rail fence just in time to avoid being run over by a company of white soldiers on horseback. Their faces were grim, and the sun glinted off their guns and bayonets. They seemed to take no notice of us and they soon disappeared, leaving nothing behind but the choking clouds of swirling red dust.

Standing Turkey and I returned to the road, clouds of red dust rising from us as well as we brushed ourselves off.

"They seem determined," Standing Turkey said. "But Kooweeskoowee will defeat them."

May 17, 1838

Despite the general uncertainty, livestock still must be fed and farm chores done. Corn is now knee-high. Napoleyan escaped his stall this morning and went into the cornfield. I was sure he had trampled the corn or at least eaten some, but he had not. I believe he just did it to irritate me. He seemed to be laughing at me as I led him back to the barn. Mules!

Too busy to write during the day and now too tired this evening to write more than this.

May 25, 1838

Finally a day of rest. Yet I find it hard to put pen to paper. The hardest part of writing is finding words. It is like trying to catch fish in the river with your hands. Just when you think you have it, there is a sudden flash of fins and the quarry darts away.

I have a new book to read. It was provided me by Reverend Elizur Butler, who is both physician and missionary. He and his wife, who is expecting a child, invited me to visit them. Upon my departure, he placed this book in my hands. Though enjoyable, Reverend Butler assured me that it is not at all frivolous. For it is based upon a true story and shows how a man placed in great trouble and danger may yet overcome terrible odds and survive.

The book is Mr. Daniel Defoe's story of a castaway, *Robinson Crusoe*. His ship is destroyed by a sudden and unexpected storm, and he is cast naked upon a desert isle. Reading this tale may help me escape for a time from the deep cares that burden all.

May 26, 1838

Have just wakened to the sound of thunder. It is not yet full dawn, so I write this by candlelight. Now I hear the crack of lightning. No, it is not! It is gunfire, and the thunder is the sound of hooves pounding the roads. Now someone is shouting words of command. A fist is pounding upon our own door!!!

June 4, 1838

I now have so much to tell that I cannot dip my pen into the ink fast enough or make my fingers catch up with my words. Even though I am still sick and weak from the loss of blood, I must write. It is a miracle that I still have this journal and that I have ink and pen to use to write.

I am now one of the many held prisoner by the armies of General Scott. We are crowded like hogs into a sty inside a high wall of timbers. No roof above us but sky and what few blankets can be spread to make shades from the sun. Few blankets, indeed. Most here have no blankets at all. Indeed, many have almost no clothes on their backs. Like my mother and my sisters and I, they were dragged from their homes before sunrise and shoved at bayonet point into the night and made to run before the soldiers down the dark roads. I must pause for a moment, for I feel about to faint.

Fainting spell has passed. I was writing of that night. I pray that I shall never again experience such a night. The darkness was lit not only by the torches carried by the soldiers, but also by the brighter light of barns and houses burning. Whether by accident or design, many of our Cherokee homes were set on fire as we left them. Perhaps it was done by the soldiers. However, I remember seeing other men darting into our homes. White men, following the troops to take whatever they might steal as soon as we were gone. I do not think our own home was set on fire, but a roughly clad man with a gray beard tried to shove past the blue-eyed soldier escorting us off our porch.

To his credit, that soldier grabbed the man by the scruff of his neck and hurled him from the porch onto his backside. The would-be looter glared up at him and then scuttled off toward the barn like a gray rat.

The soldier turned to my mother. "Your husband here?" he asked.

My mother shook her head. Emily and Ruthie peered out from behind her, glaring at the soldier.

"My mother does not speak English well," I said.

The soldier turned to me. "But you do," he said. Then he looked back over his shoulder at the sound of a ruckus from the barn. Hooves banged against wood, and a man shouted in fright. Lit by the torchlight, a large shape came bucking and kicking toward us. It was Napoleyan, dragging the terrified gray-bearded thief whose hand was caught in the halter. One final kick caught the man in his side, propelling him over the fence. Then the mule was gone, galloping off into the night.

The officer sighed, reached into the pouch at his side, and pulled out a pencil and paper.

My head spun like a top. He was now asking me to write down a list of our personal property — furniture, implements, beef cattle, fodder, machinery, horses . . . mules. Was this a dream, one the Feeler could drive from my head by the burning of tobacco and prayers to the fire? Somehow I managed to give some accounting of all we owned. He wrote it down and handed me a copy, telling me to keep it as a record since government collectors would come to gather up our property and care for it.

Then he turned to my mother and looked down at her and my sisters, still in their nightdresses. "Clothing, ma'am," he said. He pointed at their feet. "Shoes, too. But be quick about it."

My mother needed no translation. She darted back into our cabin and returned with an armful of clothing, shoes for the girls, and several blankets over her shoulders. The next thing I knew, we were on the road in a crowd of people. Shoulders jostling against each other, we stumbled down the road. The blue-eyed officer had vanished. The soldiers behind us cursed and shouted to hurry us along. Some swung clubs at our backs.

"Move, damn you, Move!"

If anyone fell, they were yanked to their feet and shoved forward. My mother and sisters had vanished in the crowd. I tried to find them, but I could not. Some of the Cherokee faces around me seemed familiar, but I could not be certain who they were. It was not just the darkness and confusion — most of those faces were distorted with fear and grief. All around us was the sound of weeping and moaning, the thud of hooves and angry oaths bellowed at us. The taste of red dust and fear, the smell of burning and sweat and blood make a memory that I fear I shall never forget. Perhaps I will never sleep again without the fear that I shall wake to such terror.

"Etsi," I cried out. "Mother."

But no one answered me. Too many were crying out the names of their mothers or fathers, children or other loved ones separated from them.

A soldier has told us that we must now stop whatever we are doing and sleep. I am too weak to protest. I can write no more tonight.

June 5, 1838

This is our tenth day in the stockade camp.

I shall return to the place where I left off as we stumbled down the dark road.

I am ashamed to say that when I realized I did not have my journal with me, I felt almost as great a fear for it as for my mother and sisters. I had left it behind in our house! It would surely be thrown away or burned.

I turned back to get it. I tried to force my way back through the crowd. I almost reached the soldiers on horseback. I hoped to find that blue-eyed officer. In my confused state, I believed he would listen to me and allow me to go back to get my journal.

Suddenly, something came hurtling down at me. It was the butt of a rifle swung by a soldier in the uniform of a United States Regular. It struck me full in the face. I heard the crunch of teeth splintering from that terrible blow that hit me like a lightning bolt. My mouth filled with blood as I staggered back.

Somehow I did not fall, but continued on. My hands were pressed to my face, blood dripping from between my fingers. Someone, I do not know who, produced a kerchief and helped me force it into my mouth to stem the flow of blood. The gentle hands of other Cherokee people, as full of loss and grief as I was, reached out with a kindness that somehow survived in the midst of chaos. They supported me, kept me from falling, helped me continue our sad journey. On we went, on toward the darkest dawn I have ever known.

Once again, I am compelled to stop for things are aspin about me.

June 7, 1838

Although my last entry was dated June 4, I must confess I am not certain what the actual date was. Within this prison we have no more access to newspapers or calendars than do cattle. Penned-up cattle, however, are better treated than Cherokees. Hundreds of us are crowded together here. I will take an exact count after I finish this entry.

Reverend Butler, who has chosen to be here among us, tells me that today's date is June 7. In three days, it will be the Sabbath. There will be a religious service for those who choose to take part.

It was Reverend Elizur Butler's face that I saw when I first woke in this place a week ago. I had no memory of arriving here. The pain and loss of blood had quite taken away my senses. I had lain senseless for nearly three days. At least one soldier thought me dead, asking those about me to carry my body from the stockade to bury outside the walls before I started to rot. His request was refused. From what I hear now, I was guarded no less fiercely than a hurt cub by a mother bear.

"Jesse," Reverend Butler said on that day when I returned to awareness. He smiled down on me, a smile both warm and edged with sorrow. "You have come back to us."

I reached up to touch the bandages about my face and winced at the deep ache in the side of my jaw.

In a soft, whispered voice, as if aware that too loud a tone would hurt my ears, Reverend Butler explained that I had lost two teeth there, shattered by the blow. But the roots had come out cleanly, and my jaw seemed not to be broken.

Gentle fingers then grasped my hands and drew them away from my face. I recognized that touch. My mother's face appeared above me. My two sisters, Emily and Ruthie, were next to her. It was the sweetest sight I had ever seen. I had feared I would never see them again in this life.

"Gogisgi," my mother whispered, holding my hands up to her wet cheeks.

"Etsi," I whispered back, my voice hoarse and weak.

My mother pulled one of her hands away from mine and held it out toward my sister Emily. Something was placed in her hand. She held it so that I could see it, but I did not recognize it at first. Then I realized it was my journal. When my dear mother had gone back onto our house, she had wrapped it into one of the blankets.

I touched the cover of my journal with trembling fingers as my other small sister, Ruthie, showed me what she held. My quills and my ink bottle.

"Wado, my dear family," I croaked. Then I fell again into sleep.

June 11, 1838

I feel much stronger today. Reverend Butler held services yesterday. He was assisted by Reverends Jesse Bushyhead and Stephen Foreman, two Cherokee men who are preachers themselves. Now more than one in ten of those in Camp Cherokee are Christian. Yet many joined in the singing of hymns in Cherokee. All seemed lifted a little by the preachers' words of faith and hope. Half a dozen men and women professed their desire to join the faith when the meeting was done.

The preachers hope to be allowed to leave the fort, under guard, to take their new converts down to the river for baptism next Sunday. The officer of the camp seems more than a little sympathetic. He and some of the other white officers and soldiers appear saddened by what they have been forced to do. They see that we Cherokees are not wild savages, but human beings who dress and live much like their own families. I think these white men have been led to wonder if the same might happen to them someday. Is it possible that someday an army of strangers will march into their homeland, looting and burning and driving them from their land as we Indians have been driven?

June 12, 1838

Reverend Butler tells me that General Scott gave firm orders for his troops to treat the Cherokees gently. Many of his men tried to follow his orders. Not so the Georgia Volunteers. Scott was shocked to hear a group of Georgia soldiers joking about which of them would gather the most Cherokee scalps.

"What is that you say, sir?" Scott asked one of them.

"Beggin' your pardon, General," a Georgian replied, "But it is well known that them Cherokees ain't truly human."

For his own part, Scott began to doubt that the Georgians among his troops were truly Christians. For that reason, Scott ensured that every Georgian he could find was under his own direct command so that he might keep an eye on them.

June 13, 1838

Tried to assist others here in the camp but was told to wait until I was well. So I sit here in our small corner and write in my journal. I shall try to describe what life is like in the camp.

Also, I must do something else. People have seen me writing and asked what I am doing. When I tell them I am keeping a record of all that has happened, they are often eager for their stories to be told. There are so many that I cannot tell them all. But I will share a few, though I will not mention the true names of any of our Cherokee people, should this journal be read by hostile eyes. Instead I shall make up names for them to protect them. (Save for my own name, the names of white people, and the names of our well-known leaders, this is what I have been doing all along.)

June 14, 1838

Stories from the Camp

Goingsnake, an elder of seventy winters, tells me the troops arrived at his house not at dawn but just as they sat down to dinner. He refused to leave until all of his family members had been allowed to kneel and follow his lead as he prayed in Cherokee. Then, with great dignity, he rose and led his family for the last time from their home.

Struck by the Bear is — or was — a wealthy Cherokee. He owned a plantation with a dozen buildings, a large herd of beef cattle, ten fine horses, and a gristmill. Forty people lived on his plantation, not including a dozen slaves. He was riding out to survey a broken fence when he heard the sound of gunfire from his home. Coming back over the hill he saw a strange sight. His family and the other Cherokees were huddled behind an overturned wagon while two parties of white men fought each other for the possession of his home. One white man and his brothers had barricaded themselves in the living room while the other white men poured round after round of gunfire in at them.

It only ended when the soldiers, a party of Tennessee Volunteers, came riding up the road. By that time, two of the white men had killed each other, and three were seriously wounded. All of them were so worn by their pitched battle that they could only limp away without claiming any of the spoils.

"The Tennesseers came too soon," Struck by the Bear said. "If they had only waited another hour, those fool white men would have all wiped each other out."

Although Struck by the Bear was allowed to take his horses and wagons, which were used to convey other Cherokees too young, too old, or too infirm to walk to Camp Cherokee, he received only a paper accounting for the rest of his property. However, he did come away with some actual coin, having sold the corn in his mill to the army quartermaster accompanying the troops. To the credit of those soldiers, they bought what they might have simply taken. It would be needed to feed the many hungry captives.

Struck by the Bear's slaves are not here in the camp. They vanished after he left his plantation. This worries him deeply. He fears they have been taken by white men who will not treat them as human beings the way he did.

Nancy, a Cherokee woman in her middle years with a family of seven, told me that the soldiers surrounded their house at midday.

"You must go now," they said to her.

"First I will feed the livestock," she said. Then she did so.

When she got out back to the hogs, she told me, she unlatched their gate. "Don't let the soldiers or the Georgians get you," she said to them in Cherokee. As she rode away she heard a ruckus and looked back to see all her pigs heading for the woods, leaving the white men far behind them.

With tears in her eyes and a certain pride, another younger woman I shall call Rose told me what happened when the soldiers tromped into the upstairs room where she sat with her grandmother.

"Ladies," their lieutenant said. "You must leave now."

"I go nowhere," her grandmother said in English. This surprised Rose, who until then had thought her elder had no knowledge of the language. Then her grandmother simply leaned back in her chair, closed her eyes, and died.

This so moved the lieutenant in command that he ordered his men to see that the old woman was buried beneath the apple tree in their backyard before the rest of the family was moved out. He then had the ground smoothed out and leaves raked over it to conceal the grave. He also ordered one man to stay behind for a time to see that the grave was not disturbed in case someone had observed the burial.

From what John Iron, who was our local Cherokee blacksmith, told me, it is well that the old woman's burying place was guarded. A rabble of thieves was following the soldiers like jackals behind a lion. Not content with simply stripping the houses of their contents, they were raiding Cherokee graves to collect the silver ornaments buried with our dead. John Iron was with a group of captives who passed by one of our burying places. He saw no fewer than a dozen white men with shovels and picks in that cemetery, digging hard and eager to rob our graves.

June 17, 1838

Under light guard, by permission of the officer in command, ten Cherokees went to the river and were baptized. It was a solemn and impressive service. The whites in attendance were much moved.

June 20, 1838

Reverend Butler is among those who have attempted to call attention to our suffering in this camp and the dozen or so others throughout what was once our Nation. He obtained a copy of the order sent on June 17 by General Scott in response to the accounts being circulated that we were poorly attended. Here are Scott's words:

> *It is, I learn, reported that throughout this country, the Indians collected in camps for emigration*

are sickly and dying in great numbers. I mention this to contradict it. The Indians are very generally in good health, and so are the troops. Please cause this to be officially announced.

In spite of General Scott's order, three died today in our camp. Two baby girls and an elderly Negro woman. I assisted in their burial. It was difficult to break the hard, dry earth.

JUNE 25, 1838

Those held in our camp number, as I count them today, 638. But it is hard to keep an accurate count. In these few weeks seventeen have died. Most were infants and old people. The weakest among us are the first to perish. More Cherokees are being driven in each day, collected from the further points of our nation.

Some who arrived today told of being herded across the Chickamauga River. Though we go to the water at the start of any of our old ceremonies, the rivers are known to also be places of danger. Our old tales speak of water monsters such as the Uktena, who hide beneath the surface and drag down the unwary. The river must always be approached with care and respect. But, at the

Chickamauga, there was no time for care. Bayonets and clubs and curses were at their backs. A dozen Cherokees drowned in that crossing.

Another group was brought all the way from North Carolina, forced to walk more than two hundred miles beneath the boiling sun. A number of them could not keep up with the line of march and fell behind. One man told of hearing rifle shots behind him as these stragglers were dispatched by impatient soldiers.

It seems that not one Cherokee will be allowed to remain. The land must be cleansed of us like soil washed from a pale hand. I am much discouraged today, and my jaw is swollen and aching greatly.

My mother has given me herbs gathered from the forest. I am to chew them and pack them into my sore gums. The officer in charge of the camp allows the women to leave the camp to get firewood and gather food plants if they promise to return. He has learned that he can always trust any Cherokee to come back once they have made such a promise. Tomorrow, if I feel better, I shall describe what it is like in Camp Cherokee. It is not a good place.

June 30, 1838

I did not feel better the next day. I had a fever and was insensible. My mother bathed my forehead with cool cloths and held me in her arms as I shivered from the cold. Somehow she managed to make a soup and feed it to me.

Food is a problem here in Camp Cherokee. On first arrival, many of our people refused to accept the government food. The children, with their pitiful cries of hunger, were the first to eat. After a few days, there was not enough. The traders given the contracts to provide food for us provide less than they are paid for, or deliver spoiled food that cannot be eaten. Today a barrel of crackers was opened. All were blue with mold. Even the hungriest of us could not eat them. Also, some of the unspoiled rations are strange to our people who are used to fresh food from their farms or the forest.

My mother tells me that a sack of coffee beans was given to some of our people who had not seen coffee before. Instead of grinding the beans to make a drink, they took the coffee beans and boiled them and tried to eat them. Those who ate that bitter soup became very sick.

It is also hard to cook with the white flour, which is not at all like ground corn. Here again, some of our women tried cooking the flour into a soup. The result was impossible to eat. Were it not for those like my mother who gather from the surrounding countryside the wild foods, people would be starving here.

July 1, 1838

More of my strength has returned. I was well enough to walk about today. So I shall describe this place. We are within a great stockade pen with high walls and no roof. One could throw a stone from one side to the other, but more than seven hundred people are now kept in here. It is hard to walk without tripping over someone's outthrust legs as they try to sleep, often on the bare ground. Some have made rude shelters from sticks and bark, using blankets to make walls for their tiny huts set up helter-skelter. People are trying their best to help each other.

There is much courtesy, yet also much despair. It is not just the heat and crowding. It is not just the fact that the very young and the very old grow weaker each day. It is also the uncertainty.

This is only one of dozens of camps and forts and collection points set up throughout our Nation. Many here have been separated from their loved ones. Some were taken captive as they walked upon the roads or worked in their fields. Others saw their children run and hide in the woods while they themselves were marched away. To his great credit as a Christian, the officer in charge has allowed some of those parents to go out on parole to seek their lost children, giving them a certain amount of time for their search.

Though we are in captivity, it is still a Sunday. The Christian ministers among us, both Cherokee and white, held services. But my walk so tired me that I was unable to attend.

July 2, 1838

Still no rain has fallen. The sun burns down upon us. The heat of so many bodies crowded together makes it hard to breathe at times. To get drinking water, we must go to the river. The water in the river has grown lower.

The water is so low that the plan of sending all our people west by boat no longer seems possible, according to one young Tennessee soldier who stops to speak with me now and then. We have learned which of the soldiers we must avoid — the ones who tend to abuse our people with words or subtle blows. This young Tennessean is not one of them. Though rough-hewn, he treats every Cherokee with courtesy.

His name is Will. I believe that he is about my own age and in some ways he reminds me of my friend Otter, whose own English name was William. Perhaps it is the way this young white man turns to look sideways at me or the way he moves his hands that makes me think of my lost friend. Because of that resemblance, I have taken to calling him White Will. At another time or another place he and I might have been friends.

White Will told me today that his father fought at the Horseshoe and other battles in the War of 1812. The Cherokees were always by his side or leading the charge against the enemy.

"Pa said the Cherokees was the bravest and the best men there," White Will said.

"What are we now?" I asked him.

His face became as red as a boiled crawfish, and he walked quickly away.

July 3, 1838

White Will sought me out today as I sat with my journal in my lap. Here there is little to do but sit. Somehow, that sitting makes me more weary than the work about our farm ever did. I am so tired that it is hard to lift this pen.

"Are ye writin' about what it be like hereabouts?" White Will asked.

I held out my journal to him. "You can read what I have said if you like."

His face turned that same crimson hue again, and he

shook his head. He looked around to see if anyone else could hear us and then crouched down beside me to tell me that he could not read a word. Nor write, neither, he added, though that was scarcely necessary.

I said nothing in return. What could I say?

White Will stood up. I stood with him. There was something on his mind other than a confession of illiteracy. Leaning close and still whispering, he asked if he might ask a favor of me. "I shall give ye favor for favor in return," he added quickly.

"Yes?" I said.

He then asked if I might help him write to his ma and pa, putting down what he said onto paper. In return he would tell me more about how things were hereabouts, things I could put down into my book. Then he thrust out a hand. "Deal?" he asked.

"Deal," I said, and we shook on it.

White Will's Letter
July 3, 1838

Dear Ma and Pa,

I am writing you this letter from the camp. Actually, I am not writing it myself. A friend is helping me with the writing down of it. He is an educated man and knows a lot. I know you are not reading this yourselves. I expect that you have gotten the preacher or Mr. Redfern at the store to do the reading aloud. Whoever is helping by reading this aloud, I do thank you most kindly.

Now that I am writing, I am not sure I have much to say except that I am well and that this is awful hard duty. It is not fair what is happening here. Some days it makes me feel like I want to cry for these poor folks who are Indian but are living just like we do. That is, they were living that way before we drove them off of their farms. Some of them are even Baptists like us. Doesn't that beat all? They have services every Sunday, so you don't have to worry about my not remembering church here. Their singing is very fine.

Tomorrow we shall celebrate our Day of Independence. I wish I could be at home to see the parade.

I hope that I will be able to come home soon.

Your loving son,
Private William Bertram

July 4, 1838

Today was their Independence Day. It was not ours.

July 5, 1838

Things White Will has told me:

1. More than 9,000 Cherokees are now in the camps.
2. The army brought in a good many of them, but far more came in peacefully on their own because our chiefs told them to do so.
3. Some other places where Cherokees are being held are Rattlesnake Spring (about 600), Mouse Creek (about 2,500), Bedwell Springs (about 1,000), Gunstocker Spring (2,000 or so), Chetooee (1,300), about 700 here and 700 or more on the ridge east of the agency.
4. About 3,000 Cherokees have been transported west since 1835, counting those sent last year and two parties this spring.
5. The rivers are getting so low that it will be hard to send more by boat.
6. General Scott acted in too great a haste to gather us up. The secretary of war had agreed to John Ross's request that we be allowed to at least get our crops in first.

> Secretary of War Poinsett sent General Scott guidelines. The Cherokees were only to be collected just before they were to be transported. October, when the summer's heat was past, was the best time to do that. It took Poinsett's letter two weeks to get to Scott. By then he had already gathered most of us into the camps and could not release us.

I asked White Will how it was that he knew so much. He did not turn crimson this time, but his voice was gruff as he said, "I be not able to read, but m' Pa taught me ter be a good listener."

Because his duties include serving the officer in charge, White Will has overheard all of these things.

July 6, 1838

I have never understood better why mosquitoes and biting flies were one of the plagues of Egypt. They are so plentiful in the air that one cannot draw a breath without swallowing half a dozen of them. Wherever one's skin is not protected by clothing, one is covered with lumps from their bites.

The smell of Camp Cherokee is that of a swamp. Though we have tried to keep our quarters clean, it is hopeless with so many and so many sick. Each day, more are carried out to be placed in the earth in shallow graves. No Cherokee can own any of this land except in death, and it is so often the very young and the very old. If we survive, we may be a Nation without children or elders.

July 7, 1838

News of the last of the three parties sent west under guard this June. A small group of Cherokees on that journey tried to run away. They were finally recaptured in the woods near here and brought to our camp. All were near starved, bruised, bleeding from wounds sustained in their flight. One of their number was so determined to not be sent west again that he had hurled himself over a cliff to avoid capture.

Some had been so beaten by the soldiers who captured them that the poor wretches suffered broken bones, though their only resistance was to run, not fight. General Scott's orders to his men may have forbade unkindness to our people, but a good part of his troops have paid no attention to such commands.

July 8, 1838

I am thankful for the health of my mother and sisters and for my own health. But I am not thankful for the salt pork. Or the water they give us to drink. We do not drink the foul water as some do, but persist in only drinking water after it has been boiled. We cook all our food with care. My mother says the sickness comes from the water and the bad food and that cooking it will kill the sickness. Her words are echoed by the white missionaries who act as doctors, but not everyone listens.

Twelve died this week past. One was a woman in childbirth. The baby also perished. Among those twelve who died was one white child, the infant daughter of Reverend Butler. Most of the children still alive have whooping cough.

July 9, 1838

Fourkiller's Story

Fourkiller is a light-skinned man in his late thirties. His blue eyes are evidence of the Scotsman who was his grandfather. He had a good job working in DeKalb County for the new Western & Atlantic Railroad along with fifty or more other Cherokees. Blue eyes or not, he had a Cherokee name and was taken from his work to be imprisoned in a camp.

He is one of those who survived escape and recapture.

His aim was to reach the hills and mountains of North Carolina, where there are many caves and deep woods to hide him. Also the Oconoluftee Cherokees live there. They are citizens of North Carolina and as such have not been compelled to give up their homes. It is rumored that others of our people, especially those poorer Cherokees most removed from white ways, have already sought refuge in the mountains. When someone here in Camp Cherokee, which many of our people now call "Camp Captured," tells of a missing family member, it is sometimes said that the person must have escaped to the hills. They are safe in the hills, we say. They are held by the hills. Yet I know that most of them must in fact be numbered among the dead.

Fourkiller's group, over a thousand Cherokees, left by wagon on June 17. All went fairly well until they reached Waterloo, Alabama, where they were told to climb on board the flatboats. They knew of the awful conditions onboard those flatboats. They had no wish to starve and suffer in that way.

"Three hundred of us threw down our baggage and took to the woods," Fourkiller said. Then he laughed. "In the woods those white men were like little children. If we had wanted we could have knocked them over the head and taken their weapons as they stumbled through the brush."

Fourkiller has now changed his plans. He will no longer make for North Carolina. Instead, when he escapes again he will find laborer's clothing and make his way back to DeKalb County, where his old job awaits him.

"I will call myself John Campbell," Fourkiller said. "They will not send a Scotsman to the Indian Territories."

July 10, 1838

Four more men and three women were baptized today. One of the women had lost both her infants to the fevers. She wept with joy at the thought that she would see them again in the life to come. I wept also, but not from joy. There are so many losses every day that the flow of our tears must now equal that of the waters of Babylon, where the exiled Israelites sat down. It is hard not to lose myself in sorrow and give up as have some of our people. My pen is like a lifeline that I must hold lest I, too, be washed away. So I continue to write.

Our good ministers are now worried that they have been too successful. So many wish to attend their services that they have begun building a small place of worship outside the stockade wall. However, it is rumored that some of those white men who are higher up wish to punish them. The white men who come into the compound almost every day to sell whiskey have complained about the Christians. The Indian Christians among us have taken oaths that they shall not drink and they shall encourage others to avoid spirituous liquor. Many of our people, who have seen the wounds we inflict upon ourselves and others when we are drunk, agree with them. This is not good for the business of the whiskey sellers.

July 11, 1838

White Will has given me two things today, and I have written another letter for him. He also asked me about our Cherokee ball game, having learned from someone that I was regarded as a great ballplayer. We talked for some time about the game. Both of us almost forgot where we were until the time came for the guard to be changed and our numbers counted to see if any had escaped.

The first thing White Will brought was news. The delegation sent by our chiefs to General Scott was successful. No further removals will take place until the fall. Also, John Ross has returned from Washington and is visiting each of the camps. He will be here at Camp Captured this coming week.

The second thing was a copy of General Scott's orders to his troops that were posted on May 17, 1838. I have mentioned them before in this journal, but now with this copy at hand I can record them exactly. Here is what Old Fuss and Feathers wrote:

ORDERS. NO.25
HEAD QUARTERS, EASTERN DIVISION
CHEROKEE AGENCY, TEN. MAY 17, 1838

The Cherokees, by the advances which they have made in christianity & civilization, are by far the most interesting tribe of Indians in the territorial limits of the United States, of the 15,000 of these people who are now to be removed — (& the time within which a voluntary emigration was stipulated, will expire on the 23rd instant) — it is understood that about four fifths are opposed, or have become averse to a distant emigration; & altho' none are in actual conflict with the United States, or threaten a resistance by army, yet the troops will probably be obliged to cover the whole country they inhabit in order to make prisoners & to march or to transport the prisoners, by families, either to this place, to Ross' Landing or Gunter's Landing, where they are to be finally delivered to the Superintendent of Cherokee Emigration . . .

. . . Every possible kindness, compatible with the necessity of removal, must, therefore, be shown by the troops, &, if, in the ranks, a despicable individual should be found, capable of inflicting a wanton injury or insult on any Cherokee man, woman or child, it is hereby made the special duty of the near-

> est good officer or man, instantly to interpose, & to seize & consign the guilty wretch to the severest penalty of the laws.

I read Scott's orders aloud to White Will, who said he could recollect having heard them before. At the time they did not have much meaning for him and so he had mostly forgot them. He would, by God, remember them now.

July 12, 1838

Today I woke up from a dream. I was standing near the hollow tree where I had hidden my father's musket. The Feeler was there with me. He had something in his hand. It was wrapped in the deerskin I had given him. He held it out, showed it to me, then placed it deep within the tree.

It is the first time I have dreamed pleasantly since coming to this place. It was good to see my great-uncle in that dream. I have spent much of the day thinking about him. Dreams are of great importance to our people. Was this dream a message?

July 13, 1838

Chief John Ross visited the camp and spoke to the people. He did not bring the best news. The best news would have been that we could return to our homes. That can never be again. Our homes and lands are now firmly in the hands of white men. I am sorry for our homes and lands. I have not seen it, but some of those on the camp allowed passes to seek their lost children have. They say that many of those who have taken our homes seem to be poor housekeepers and have no respect for the living earth. This land will suffer without us.

But the news spoken by Chief Ross was, to some small degree, good news. Though short in stature, when Tsan Usdi speaks, he draws himself up and seems tall as a great oak. He is not an orator like the Ridge, but speaks with such honest certainty that no one doubts his words.

"We may be allowed to conduct our own removal," Tsan Usdi said in his soft, clear voice. "Instead of rough white men with guns forcing us along the trail, we may be led by other Cherokees. We shall not have to travel the dangerous rivers or be placed on the roaring trains. Too many precious lives were lost that way. Instead, we may go by land, departing when the fall rains arrive, cooling the land and making travel easier than in the killing summer heat."

Chief Ross also spoke of the whiskey traders who prey upon us like vultures on weak lambs. He urged us to drive them out. General Scott has given his blessing to that effort. To that I say, Hurrah!

July 14, 1838

Another Sunday and the singing in our morning services seemed more joyful. John Ross's words have given new spirit to us.

A number of us in good health have begun making shelters for those too weak to build their own. Our leader is a full-blood named Sam Blackfox, who is a member of the General Council.

We have also formed a group to enforce temperance in the camp. With the help of three sympathetic soldiers (White Will among them), the whiskey traders were ejected from the compound this morning. Since the traders were white men, we Cherokees were unable to force them out. One whiskey trader tried to stand his ground. But the three soldiers gave that man a good beating. All his jugs were smashed. The two other traders escaped as quickly as they could in their wagon. I think they will not come back soon.

July 16, 1838

I was not well. I woke two days ago coughing and spitting blood. It frightened me. I have seen this happen to others just before they give up the ghost. My mother remained calm and soothed me. The wound in my jaw where my teeth were knocked out had begun to bleed. The blood was clean, she said. I would be weak for a spell, but I would be healthy again in a day or so. Then she fed me soup made from greens she gathered. Today I feel strong. For the first time since I was struck by the gun butt, my jaw does not ache.

A party of a dozen Cherokees, mostly men, came in today from the hills to the east. They received the call from John Ross to surrender. All were well armed but gave up their guns to the soldiers with the promise their weapons would be returned as soon as they were safely on the other side of the Mississippi.

July 19, 1838

John Ross has called for a General Council meeting on July 21. General Scott has approved it. He is allowing parole to a few Cherokee men chosen by our people to represent us. They may leave the camps if they pledge to only attend the meeting at the Aquohee Stockade and then return. Scott has learned that though a Cherokee may run away when he has the chance, he will never break his word.

Among those in the camp who will go to Aquohee is Sam Blackfox. He has asked me to accompany him as his secretary.

July 22, 1838

My heart is full. Though in bondage, we are yet a nation. Our people resolved at Aquohee that the business of emigration would be undertaken by our Nation. Chief John Ross will be the superintendent. He will negotiate with Washington to obtain funds to pay for the journey of eight hundred miles that will take eighty days to complete.

I did not speak in the Council, since I was only attending as a clerk. However, my mother saw that I was well dressed for the occasion. In the camp, our clothes have been reduced to rags. Some of our people are almost naked. Living without proper shelter and with no easy means to wash ourselves or our laundry has also been hard upon our garments. It is not uncommon to see shirts and dresses made of blankets and various pieces of cloth sewn together. Somehow, with the help of others who heard I would go to Red Clay, proper clothing was put together for me. I was given a blue-and-white shirt. Though a size too large, it was without a single patch or tear. Someone supplied a beautiful piece of red-patterned cloth that I wore about my head in a Cherokee turban. For many years now the turban has been the favorite head covering for Cherokee men. Some white men see our turbans as proof of their theory that our ancestors came from far across the ocean to the east and that we are the descendants of Hindoos. They have also credited us as one of the missing Tribes of Israel, a nation of wandered Jews. When I spoke of those theories to the Feeler, he laughed for a long time.

When I emerged from our little lean-to of poles and blankets, I found Sam Blackfox waiting. He looked me up and down and nodded in approval. He, too, was well dressed. Also he had found four turkey feathers to place in his turban. We walked toward the gate and it opened before us. For the first time in many weeks I found myself looking at the horizon and not the rough wooden walls of a stockade. I felt quite giddy, but managed not to stumble.

A wagon had been loaned by the army to convey us to Red Clay and back again. The horses, however, were balking and unruly. Upon seeing that, Sam Blackfox climbed up onto the seat and requested the driver to climb down, which he did. Sam Blackfox then took the reins and made a clucking noise with his tongue. The horse pricked up their ears and set off.

It was a surprise to some of the soldiers who were watching, but it was no surprise to me. The wagon was a Cherokee wagon. The horses were Cherokee horses. Before he was taken from his home and stripped of all he owned, that wagon and horses belonged to Sam Blackfox.

When we returned from Aquohee, Blackfox handed

the wagon back over to the army men. He then pressed his face against the cheek of each of those two horses in turn, whispering something to them. Then, though I know not from where he got them, he produced two sugar cubes and gave one to each horse. For some reason there were tears in my eyes as we walked back into the stockade. I found myself remembering our cussed old mule Napoleyan.

For the first time, there will be much to do here. I will try to put down the main points of the council meeting in my journal as time permits.

July 30, 1838

Chief Ross turned in his estimation of expenses for our emigration. It amounts to about $65 per person to remove the remaining 12,000 of our people who are in the stockade camps. Thus far, General Scott has informed him, the army has spent $600,000 for the expenses of feeding and housing us and for the spring removals. This $600,000 has already been deducted from the monies set aside to pay us for our land in the Treaty of New Echota. The costs of emigration will also be deducted from the treaty monies.

All of this information has been made public by Superintendent Ross at the General Council.

August 2, 1838

General Scott agreed that horses, oxen, and wagons should be provided for our removal. He has said that one wagon and five saddle horses for each twenty people would be satisfactory. There should be among the Cherokees at least five hundred strong men, women, boys, and girls capable of marching twelve to fifteen miles a day. The exercise would be good for them. That is what Scott said.

August 3, 1838

John Ross responded to Scott's offer. Our chief pointed out that our wagons will be loaded heavily with cooking utensils, bedding, and other items needed for twenty people. With that much weight, no more than a few persons could be hauled. Scott agreed to this logic. There shall be at least one team, one wagon, and six riding horses for every fifteen people.

August 8, 1838

Have just returned to Camp Cherokee after four days away. A number of us have been given parole to gather horses and wagons for the emigration. Some of the agents sent out to gather the necessities for our emigration are independent contractors or with the army. But they have also allowed some Cherokees passports to take part in this effort as long as we have at least one white soldier keeping us company. Most often our agents must buy back property and livestock taken from us illegally. The brother of Chief Ross, Lewis Ross, is handling all of the monies for the emigration, and we have been given a budget to obtain transport. Each horse is being branded with the letters CN. This stands for Cherokee Nation.

Despite the fact that our emigration cannot begin until the fall, General Scott insists that our people remain in the camps. There is enough food to keep us from starving. There are now a few more blankets. But there is still much suffering. There is no good sanitation for so many people. Although pit latrines have been dug away from the walls, there is always a bad smell from human waste and from sickness. While I was away, eight more people died in Camp Cherokee. Among the dead were the sister and the infant son of Sam Blackfox, who led our party.

August 9, 1838

Hard work this past Tuesday and Wednesday. Reverend Bushyhead has been given permission to move the Cherokee Baptist Church. The white man who is the owner of the land wants no church upon it, but has shown some decency by allowing the reverend to take what he can of it to Indian Territory. If it were possible, Reverend Bushyhead would take every stone, shingle, and board. But he has decided to be content with taking only those things most easily portable. The sole exception is that which caused us such labor. We have been removing the heavy beams, all six of them. They shall hold up the roof of the Cherokee Baptist Church when it rises again on our new lands.

I found myself in the group of laborers disassembling the church. Sam Blackfox, who is Baptist, asked if I might have the time to help a little. Since the death of Sam's sister and his son, whose graves Sam insisted upon digging with his own hands, he has worked twice as hard as before. He must stop often because of a racking cough that shakes his whole body. There was no way I could refuse him.

The white soldiers who went with us as our guards also joined in the labor. Though the soldiers at some of the camps have been cruel to our people, more often than not I have found them to be decent men like my friend White Will. Though some were stern to us at first, they now appear to have grown to like or respect us. Many, in fact, are quite ashamed of what has been done to the Cherokees.

By the end of the second day of our labors, Reverend

Bushyhead — who rolled up his sleeves and worked beside us — was joking with me. My name should not be the same as his, he said. Rather than Jesse, I should be renamed Samson, for my strength was helping to bring down the temple.

I joked in return that perhaps his name should be Solomon, for was he not going to raise up the temple of the Lord?

Though I am not a Baptist, Reverend Bushyhead enjoys conversing with me. I know the Bible as well as any, and he is one who much enjoys intelligent conversation. Only a week ago we had a lively discussion on the supposition that Christ could not have been a white man but must, in fact, have been an Indian or at the very least one whose spirit was more like that of our own people. Few white men seem to value generosity over the possession of material things.

Upon returning to our small corner of noisome Camp Cherokee, I asked my mother, bent over a pot of squirrel stew hung above our little cooking fire, if she had noted any change in me. Did I appear larger and stronger? She allowed that I had, indeed, grown at least the width of two fingers in height. Despite the poor food in the camp, my shoulders had broadened.

"You look much like your . . . ," she said. Then my

mother turned quickly back to her cooking without finishing her words. But not before I saw the tears in her eyes like those that blurred my own vision.

August 12, 1838

I attended the services led by Reverend Jesse Bushyhead today to say farewell to Sam Blackfox. He died this morning. I helped Reverend Bushyhead dig the grave. After the burial was over I sat, for how long I did not know, with one hand pressed against the soft earth as if I could again hold my friend's strong hand one last time. It was not easy to find the strength to stand.

How hard it is to make new friends and then lose them. Some of our people now seem to have closed their eyes to the living. They wait only for the sight of their dead loved ones who will come to them and embrace them when they, themselves, have passed from this earth and gone to the next world.

Fourteen died this week.

August 16, 1838

I have been reunited with a dear old friend. He is stubborn as ever. Still, my mother and my sisters and I are delighted that we shall be sharing his company. I am speaking of Napoleyan, our red mule. We did not purchase him, as we have had to do with the other animals we have been gathering for our exodus. Instead, he joined our company quite on his own.

Yesterday, as we rode past cabins that had once been Cherokee and now were inhabited by white families, a white man with a black beard came out to hail us. The newly arrived white farmers have begun to be much more friendly to us now that they see us with ready cash in our pockets for the purchase of horses and oxen.

This man, however, did not have a horse or an ox to sell. Instead he had a request. "If you is looking for animals," he said with considerable eagerness, "there's a mule that has been tromplin' our fields. It would gratify us if you was to take him, free of charge. Or even kill him for the meat."

He then spoke fervently about the great red devil that came at night to his fields. It kicked down their fences and flattened their corn with its great hooves, devouring whatever it felt like. They had tried to shoot it, but it was too elusive for them and would take to the piney woods before any of them could catch it.

Though my face showed no mirth during his disquisition, I must confess that I was smiling inwardly. The crops that the "red devil" had been trampling had been planted not by these white farmers but by Cherokees. I had a good idea just who that mule was. We were but a few miles from the farm that had been my family's.

Arrow Toter, the Light Horse leader of our troop, looked over at me and nodded. It was Arrow Toter who had waved to me that day last November as his men galloped past our farm. He thanked the farmer and said that we would keep a lookout. As soon as we had rounded the bend, Arrow Toter turned to me. "The mule is yours?" he said to me in Cherokee.

"It sounds like him," I answered.

Arrow Toter laughed. "If only such creatures could have offspring," he said, "then we might leave them here to share their blessing with generations of whites to come."

"If only," I agreed.

"Call him," Arrow Toter said.

So, as we rode along, I called to Napoleyan. I did not shout his name. Instead, I brought his memory to my mind. I saw again those times when we were together. I saw myself as a small boy crawling beneath him. I put the pictures into my thoughts of currying him with the brush, taking him to the creek for water, bringing him oats, scratching behind his ears with my right hand as I fed him a carrot.

My eyes were closed as I rode, picturing those good memories. I do not know for how long. Time goes away when you remember in such a fashion.

I heard the sound of hooves coming up beside me at the same time that a wet nose was pressed against my hand.

Though he much prefers the company of Indians, Napoleyan remains a cussed mule. He came to me as gentle as a lamb and suffered me to comb the tangles from his mane. He stood as I treated the cuts and other wounds upon his side, including one that will leave a scar and seemed to be the graze of a bullet. But it was quite another matter when they tried to burn the CN mark into his rump. He kicked the red-hot brand from John Iron's hand and then chased him twice around the corral before poor John was able to escape. Napoleyan will go west on his own terms, free of the brand of the Cherokee Nation.

August 18, 1838

The Cherokees held at the other camps and stockades throughout what was once our Nation are all brought west to make ready for our departure. Our wagon trains will set out from the Cherokee Agency.

Among the new arrivals was a painfully thin young woman of my age. She was wandering about, looking quite lost. My mother saw that her dress had once been a fine one, though now it was ragged and unmended. She rose and took her by the hand and brought her to our small fire. Then my mother began to comb her tangled hair. Quite overcome by this kindness, this poor young girl, whom I shall call Betsy Redbird, poured out the terrible story of what had happened to her at the fort where she had been held captive.

She and her friends were returning from Mission School when they were taken captive still far from their homes. They were brought to the camp where none of them had relatives. A group of young white soldiers soon began speaking to her and her friends. The girls had a good command of English. They were dressed and comported themselves quite like proper young white ladies. At first, the soldiers treated them with what seemed to be great courtesy and respect. At their lonely post, far from other young women of their own race, those white soldiers seemed to view the Cherokee lasses much as they would their own sisters and sweethearts at home.

One night this changed. Several of those young soldiers came to them with bottles of spiritous liquor and induced them to drink. By now these girls had been in that camp for many weeks and had viewed far too much suffering and death. They were in some despair. In those inhuman surroundings, every one of them had seen people die.

"The worst," Betsy Redbird said, "was to see the babies die. We wanted to forget the babies."

Although it went quite against the temperance teachings of their schooling, the girls began to drink with the soldiers. Perhaps they thought that drinking would for a time take them away from their sordid surroundings. They could pretend they were at a cotillion, listening to waltz music and discussing literature.

When the girls had become almost insensible with drink, the soldiers began to pull them away from the fire. They tried to resist, but were too weak and too drunk. They cried out for help, but the soldiers were armed. The Cherokee men who tried to come to their aid were driven back with curses and blows as the girls were dragged out of the camp into the darkness.

I said nothing as Betsy told us her story, her eyes upon the fire as she spoke. My mother put her arms around the poor girl. My two sisters held her hands as she wept and wept. A fierceness filled my heart, a great anger at all that had caused this to happen to our people. Had a gun been in my hand and Old Hickory before me at that moment, I think I would have discharged the weapon into his chest.

Yet as much as I felt hatred at that moment for the white people whose greed led to our downfall, I felt even more toward those Cherokees who betrayed us. They had signed the fraudulent Treaty of New Echota that agreed to our removal. Those traitorous men and their families were already in Indian Territory, having gone ahead of us.

They had been treated with deference by the army. Now they were likely building comfortable new houses, having selected the best of the western land for themselves.

Then another thought came to me. What would happen when the rest of our Nation arrived, including those who now saw them as blood enemies? Though it was not a cold night, a shiver went down my spine.

I lifted my head and saw that Betsy was now looking at me across the fire. I reached out my hand and placed it gently upon hers. "You are most welcome to stay with us," I said.

August 23, 1838

Our chiefs have divided our people into emigration parties of about one thousand each. As far as possible, the parties are made up of relatives and friends and neighbors. Aside from one group, we will have no soldiers guarding us. That group is partly made up of the remaining Cherokees who are pro-treaty and opposed to Chief John Ross. They number less than seven hundred and will be given a military escort.

These pro-treaty Cherokees have made themselves more evident in the last few weeks. They have buzzed about like hornets, stirring up trouble. They have tried with little success to convince others to join them. They have promised more land in the west to anyone who joins them. They have offered to pay at the onset of the journey the whole of the $65 Removal payment each Cherokee is allotted. Those who travel with our loyal Cherokees will receive half that money as we set out, and the other half when we reach the west.

They have also said, which is a dirty lie, that Chief John Ross and his family will make a great profit from his contract with the government.

All this has made the general mood even more grim.

Eight deaths in the last two days.

August 28, 1838

Although the deadline set by Scott was September 1, we hope to begin our sad trek before then. Despite the heat and lack of rain, the first emigration detachment has begun to move for departure. It is led by Hair Conrad; 729 people.

John Ross will not depart until the last of our people are safely upon their way.

September 1, 1838

No rain.

Detachment led by Elijah Hicks set out today — 43 wagons, 430 horses. With him is White Path, one of the most beloved of our old chiefs. White Path is most infirm. Many people still lack clothing, blankets, etc. Some families do not even have a single cooking pot to prepare their food.

Twelve more died this week.

September 3, 1838

Reverend Bushyhead's detachment left today — 950 people.

September 4, 1838

Many now ill with measles. It is a terrible disease for Indians. Most whites survive it. Most often we do not. To our children it is frequently fatal, but those who contract this spotted sickness as adults nearly always die.

By a strange twist of fate, our family has already experienced this plague. My mother had measles when a small girl. It swept through her family, killing her relatives. She alone recovered. As for me, I caught it while at boarding school. Not knowing that I had it, I came home, became gravely ill, and infected my sisters. My mother nursed us back to health. Knowing how deadly this plague was to Cherokees, my mother warned off our sympathetic neighbors by tying red-and-white cloths to sticks and fastening them at each corner of our fence. Still, we were given help. Many people left food by our fence but never came within sight of any of us until we had recovered.

Now my fears are for others. How many will die from this new affliction?

September 8, 1838

Still no rain.

More detachments have set out on the trail. Among them is the party of emigrants led by Situwakee — 1,250 Cherokees from the Valley Towns of east Tennessee; 62 wagons and 560 horses. The kind Reverend Evan Jones is with this party.

I find myself thinking today about my friend Reverend Jesse Bushyhead. His wife is expecting a child and will certainly give birth before they reach the western lands. My mother is worried for her, but Reverend Bushyhead has faith that the Lord will take care of his own. Also his sister, Otahki, is traveling with them and will be there to help his wife.

Otahki has two young children of her own. She is regarded by everyone as a kind and caring person. Her husband, Lew Hildebrand, will be acting as a courier for John Ross. My mother is especially fond of her friend "Nanny." That is her special name for Otahki. When Otahki's first husband, John Walker, was murdered in 1834, my mother was one of those who comforted Nanny, as Nanny did her on my own father's death.

Reverend Bushyhead has not failed to conduct services on a single Sunday, despite the hardship of the camps. Even when he and Reverend Evan Jones made their journey east this summer at Scott's request to try to convince the Cherokees in the mountains of North Carolina to come in, he managed to keep the Sabbath.

Before he left, I spoke again to Reverend Bushyhead about the great anger I have felt in my heart at the pro-treaty Cherokees.

"Did not Samson," I asked, "bring down the temple onto the heads of his enemies?"

In reply, Reverend Bushyhead gently reminded me that though I might be strong, I am not Samson. True as the words of the Old Testament are, the New Testament shows that forgiving our enemies is one of the greatest of teachings. It makes the heart lighter to do so. If we do not forgive each other, our hatred will only grow until we are all destroyed.

I hope I can find the strength to forgive. My heart is so heavy now that a millstone could not weigh more in my breast.

As I walked away from our conversation I remembered something. His sister Otahki's first husband, John

Walker, was not killed by a white man. John Walker was one of the Cherokees who opposed John Ross and went to Washington to speak in favor of the treaty. He was murdered by another Cherokee.

September 12, 1838

Word has come back of the five emigration parties that have left thus far. All have had to hold up at the mouth of the Hiwassee River, Blythe's Ferry, only twenty-five miles from here. There is such great heat, and water is so scarce that their animals cannot keep going. The rivers are too low for the ferry to be operated. Still, Choowalooka's party departs tomorrow or next day. Choowalooka is known to the white men as James D. Wofford. Reverend Butler has voiced concern to me about the choice of Choowalooka. In the past, he was known to drink most heavily. Can a drunken Moses lead our Israelites? Perhaps it would be fitting, since we are not going to the Promised Land but to a place far west of Eden.

Fifteen died in the last three days.

September 15, 1838

Elizabeth has continued to stay with us. (She prefers to be called Elizabeth rather than Betsy.) Because of my mother's cooking, her face no longer looks thin as a hatchet blade. It is no longer so hard to look at her. In fact, she is better looking than I had first thought. Her voice is also pleasant. I think that the name of Redbird suits her well since its song is quite melodious.

She is watching me now as I write. Perhaps I should cross out these last few sentences. Reading them again makes me feel uncomfortable.

September 16, 1838

Greatly afeared for Emily, who has a cough. I pray it is not whooping cough but is only due to the continued dryness of weather and dust.

I am more than ready to depart and put the torch to our small rude lean-to of bark and sticks. Elizabeth helps much in caring for Emily. She has given Emily a kerchief to tie over her nose and mouth to keep out the dust.

We are all sick with worry.

September 19, 1838

Emily's cough has lessened, and she is stronger. Wearing the kerchief over her face helped her very much. It was not the whooping cough but only the dust. Today my mother and my younger sister Ruthie both embraced Elizabeth and thanked her. I nodded my agreement and then went out quickly to help in the harnessing of animals for the next party that is leaving. Because I am good with animals, this has fallen to be one of my jobs.

Good though I may be with animals, it did not stop Napoleyan from spilling me off his back today. He did not run away but merely turned and looked down at me as if to ask why I was there and not upon his back. I have a large scrape upon my left elbow. Though I speak both English and Cherokee well, I feel there are not enough words in the two languages combined to fully describe the cussedness of that blasted species that has been named the mule.

September 20, 1838

Departures have begun again with Richard Taylor's party. Fully half of our Nation are now upon the trail. They drag their feet as they walk, carrying burdens of grief so heavy that each step they take away from our beloved homeland is a great labor. Behind them they leave only heartbreak and loss; ahead there seems to be no prospect but even greater suffering.

Pro-treaty Cherokees have not yet left. They number

about seven hundred, but have gained no new recruits, even though they swear that their route will be easier than the one chosen by the loyal Cherokees.

September 23, 1838

A better day today. With so many of the Christian ministers, both white and Cherokee, now upon the trail, I wondered who would appear to lead our services upon this Sunday. To my great surprise it was Preacher Tsan. Since he has a wonderful voice, whether singing stomp dance songs or hymns of praise, the singing was the best it has been in many days.

He nodded at me when he saw me join the gathering. When services were over, he spent a good deal of time talking with my mother. She seemed as happy to see him as was I. Finally I drew Tsan away so that he and I could sit together in the shade of an oak tree.

"Where have you been?" I asked him.

Tsan told me that he had been taken by Georgia soldiers while on the road two days to the south. Surprisingly, they had shown him some respect because of his calling. They took him to a fort farther to the east and allowed him to hold services. He had been with the last group just brought here to Camp Cherokee. I told him I had been keeping my journal, and shared some of it with him. He approved of it, saying that I was doing well.

We sat for a time in silence. Then the hint of a smile played at the edge of Tsan's mouth. "I have seen your grandfather," he said.

His words stunned me. The Feeler was not dead after all! I finally managed to stammer out a response, asking in which camp he was being held.

Then Tsan smiled, a true smile this time. The Feeler was in no camp at all. The soldiers have never caught on. Instead, he has been wandering freely from one camp to another, using his medicine to help those who are sick and come to the edge of the camps for his aid. When Tsan asked him how it was that the soldiers allowed him such freedom, the Feeler answered that the white people allowed him nothing.

"They are blind," the Feeler said. "Their eyes are smaller than those of the mole. They can see no farther than their own shadows. They cannot see me."

September 26, 1838

Our claims for losses and damages have not fared well. Many of us have not yet been paid, and the money is needed for the arduous journey ahead. Governor Lumpkin is one of the two commissioners appointed to supervise and carry into effect the treaty of removal. He has always shown favor to the pro-treaty Indians, whose claims have all been paid in full. Most of us will go west with not even a partial repayment for our losses. So much for the detailed accountings given us by the army.

But neither money nor goods can ever set the balance straight. How much could be paid for the life of a husband or a wife, a mother or a father or a beloved elder? All of the gold that the white men love so dearly was not worth the loss of even one Cherokee child. So much has been torn from our hearts that I wonder if we shall ever again be whole as a people, if any Cherokee shall ever be able to look again at the setting sun without his or her eyes brimming over with tears.

I stood today by the gate looking into the woods. The earth is bare of every branch and dry twig. All have been gathered for firewood. There is no longer the sign of a squirrel, and even the birds are now few. The bows and blowguns of our hunters have taken all of the game to feed the thousands kept captive.

For a time as I stood there, the air smelled clean. Then the wind shifted and brought to me the smells of the latrines, of urine and sickness. I do not want to leave our land, but I will be glad when we depart from Camp

Captured. It has been a hell upon earth. Farewell to salt pork forever!

As I write this by lantern light I heard something spattering on the roof of our little shelter. Rain! The blessed fall rains have come at last.

September 28, 1838

My mother and my sisters and I have been chosen for a later detachment. So I have been going about saying farewell to our friends. Among those leaving today was Standing Turkey and his wife. Their family is smaller now. They lost four of their children to sickness in the camp.

It took all morning to form the line of wagons, perhaps fifty of them. I am not sure of my estimate. The wind blew dust into my eyes. It was hard at times to breathe because of the dust clouds.

Finally, at noon, all was ready. What a sight it was to behold, that long line of people and wagons stretching for a mile along the road that was edged by heavy forest. Perhaps one-fifth of the party were in the wagons or on horseback. Those in the wagons were mostly those too young, too old, or too infirm to walk upon their own feet. The rest would try to walk the whole way. Many of those on foot looked only slightly less weak or ill than those who rode. The awful summer in the camps has taken its toll on us.

Old Going Snake, one of our most respected chiefs, tapped his heel gently against the side of his pony and made his way to the head of the line. Several other young men on horses followed him. The day was now bright and beautiful, yet no one smiled up at the Great Apportioner, the sun, to give thanks for this day.

That is when a most curious thing occurred. A deep roll of thunder sounded. Not one cloud was in the sky, yet that sound rumbled up from the heart of the hills behind us. Then it was gone, leaving a perfect silence. It was as if all who were there held their breaths. Was our beloved land speaking its protest at our mistreatment? Was that thunder an omen of future troubles to be visited upon this land? I cannot say, but I marked it well. I shall not forget it.

Then that moment of silence was gone, replaced by the call to "move on," the thump and rattle of wagons, the shuffle of hundreds of feet on the dry earth.

The last familiar face I saw as they moved away was that of Standing Turkey. He turned back, put his right hand on his chest, and then held his palm out toward me. I did the same before he was lost to my sight in the dust of the hard road.

We shall meet again in the west.

October 2, 1838

We are finally on our way. We are with the party led by Old Field and assisted by Reverend Stephen Foreman. I look forward to finding time along the way to talk with Reverend Foreman, who was educated at the Union and Princeton Theological Seminaries. I noted that a box of books was among his possessions. It has been a long time since I have held a book in my hands or had the leisure to read one.

Among the Cherokee police aiding this party is my friend Arrow Toter. I am riding with him. I am not an official member of the Light Horse, but I have been given this task of assistant interpreter and courier. Many of our people speak little or no English. My education has made me useful. Arrow Toter also knows me to be reliable, and I have kept my strength, unlike many others who are too ill to help.

My mount is my red mule Napoleyan. He refuses to allow any other to ride him and will not suffer himself to be fastened into one of the teams that draw our sixty wagons.

"Two things there are that we may do with this animal," Arrow Toter said to me two days ago from the place where he lay upon his back. Napoleyan had just thrown him and was now innocently cropping a tuft of grass. "To shoot this mule and eat him is the first, which I would prefer." Arrow Toter sat up, feeling for broken bones, of which there were thankfully none. "The second, which I suppose is more practical, is that you ride him."

Among my duties, for which I will earn about twenty-five cents a day, will be to go back and forth with messages between the thirteen parties of our people. Our long line of march is now stretched out for fifty miles between here and McMinnville.

At times I may be among those who scout ahead to find camping places for the night. It is fortunate that Preacher Tsan is in our party. He can help my mother and sisters when I am not around. We expect to make no more than ten miles a day. With so many upon the road it may not be easy finding places for us to pull up our wagons and put up our tents.

October 3, 1838

White Will rode out to bid farewell. He was away from Camp Cherokee when our caravan left. He is one of the few soldiers remaining there. With some excitement he told me that he, too, would be going west. He is to be part of the detachment under Lieutenant Deas that will escort one of the emigration parties.

"Which detachment?" I asked. In truth, I already knew the answer.

"The one led by Bell," he said.

I said nothing in return. John A. Bell's émigrés are the remaining pro-treaty Cherokees who have turned their backs to John Ross. Of our thirteen detachments, theirs is the only group leaving our lands voluntarily. The Judas party.

I had tried to explain the division among our people to White Will. I told him that a small group of men led by the Ridges and Waties went to that infamous meeting at New Echota in December 1835 called by Reverend John Schermerhorn. Schermerhorn was despised by the other Christian missionaries. He had tried again and again to bypass John Ross. We Cherokees had taken to calling Schermerhorn "Sgina yona," which means "the Devil's Horn." Fewer than one hundred Cherokee came to that meeting, not one of them a legal representative of our Nation. Among them, less than twenty men signed the treaty agreeing to our removal.

Will had listened closely. I could see that he was thinking about it.

"What is a-goin' to happen to them what signed that treaty?"

I then explained to him that by signing away our lands, their lives were forfeit. They knew that when they signed they might also be signing their own death warrants.

Will looked thoughtful for a moment and then ventured the opinion that perhaps those Cherokees felt it was the best deal that could have been made.

That had ended our discussion. It was clear to me that White Will could not understand.

So, as we sat there this day, Will upon a fine black horse and me on my red mule, I made no mention of the Bell party. I would not see Will along the way, for I'd heard that their route would be far different from ours. They would head due west while we would swing in an arc to the north where there were more towns from which we could obtain the provisions needed for our thousands of exiles.

"Ye look differnt," Will said. "Ye look fine."

I looked at myself. My dress was different from that in the camp, it was true. I no longer was dressed in rags, but in serviceable clothing and boots provided to me by the conductor. I wore a sash about my waist and a turban upon my head in the same fashion as Arrow Toter. If I was to be a messenger I had to be properly attired.

Will reached inside his tunic. He brought something out and handed it to me. It was wrapped in a red cloth. I opened it to disclose a fine, long-bladed knife in a new leather sheath.

"I figgered ye could use a pigsticker," Will said.

"Hold out your hand," I said.

I then quickly placed in White Will's palm the penny I had extracted from my pocket, explaining before he might ask that it was for the knife and that it was one of our customs.

White Will carefully put the penny into his left breast pocket. He buttoned it and patted his chest once with his right hand. Then he wheeled his horse and rode away without looking back. Though he had not known that to give a friend a knife is to cut their friendship unless something is quickly returned in payment, he had clearly remembered one thing I had taught him: We Cherokees have no word for good-bye.

October 5, 1838

Crossed to north side of Hiwassee River by ferry, above Gunstocker Creek. Took all day to ferry across all our wagons.

We do not have enough tents for all those in the party. Many must sleep outside or crowd together into what tents we have when rain begins to fall.

October 6, 1838

One wagon broke down yesterday. Helped replace axletree. Road slick with rain. Hard to walk without falling. It is as if the sky weeps with us, as if the muddy earth does not wish to let us go, but seeks to hold us back. Some people keep their balance by grasping the wagons. Many are covered with mud spattered on them from the wagon wheels. Duck's Uncle, a man in his thirties who limps, almost fell beneath the rear wheel of the fifth wagon. I was riding close by and, seeing him stumble, I reached down, grasped his arm, and pulled him up. At my insistence he rode the rest of that day inside the bed of a wagon.

Too tired to write more.

October 7, 1838

Stopped for religious services. No travel today. Our movement is like that of a great army. Hundreds of wagons, thousands of horses. Some few among us are well-to-do Cherokees. They drive fine carriages and are attended by black slaves. Some of those men and women are as well dressed as any white family off to church. There are also among us white men married to Cherokee women, and white women married to Cherokee men. All are no better than Indians in the eyes of the United States, despite their wealth or dress or color of their skin.

Most of our people in this wagon train are poor. Their families have little but each other and their faith in John Ross to sustain them. When they camp at night by family groups, each lodge builds a small fire. Trenches are dug for the latrines to be used by the men on one side of the camp, while other trenches are dug on the other side for the women. Bathing areas are set aside for men and women in some nearby stream. Clothing is washed. The small evening meal is prepared and eaten. There is little conversation. Most are too exhausted or sick or dispirited to say much.

Our Light Horsemen stay at the flanks and guard our rear as we travel. We are still being harried by white men. They follow us hoping to cheat us out of what little we have, or steal what they cannot get through guile. Several of our horses have been seized by white men for payment of unjust and past demands. Also we have encountered sellers of cakes, pies, fruits, cider, applejack, and whiskey. Sharks, all eager to snatch what little cash we carry. Sadly, some of us are too ready to oblige them. The Light Horse must keep an eye out for these merchants and also keep control of those Cherokees who become drunk to forget their sorrow.

Whiskey. The bane of death.

October 9, 1838

Second ferry crossing at Blythe's Ferry over Tennessee River a short distance above Jolly's Island at mouth of Hiwassee. Ferrymen charging the Cherokee emigrants double the normal rate. They also delay each crossing as much as possible, saying they must mend the cable, make one repair or another. The ferrymen are paid by the merchants who have made camp by the river. Though our Light Horse tries to keep the whiskey sellers away, we cannot use much force against them since we are Indians and they are white men.

October 10, 1838

Our whole party took two days to cross. Were it not for the insistence of our conductor it might have taken three days. On now to McMinnville.

October 11, 1838

The hill that rises to the top of Walden Ridge was too much for most of our teams. A two-mile ascent. Had to unhitch teams from one wagon to double them up on another. Then had to bring teams back down hill to bring up the next wagon. With sixty wagons to service in this fashion, it took a great long while to bring all to the top. Rather than making ten miles a day we have been lucky thus far to make even six. Reverend Bushyhead's detachment is proceeding just as slowly. Three teams were needed to draw up the wagon with the beams of his church in its bed.

Excessive fees were charged for our party at the Walden Ridge tollgate. Charges are 37½¢ for four wheeled carriages and 6½¢ for each horse or ox. At least $40 for each of our detachments. Is there no end to the greed of those who are not merely satisfied with taking our land but seem to wish to drain us of our very blood?

October 12, 1838

Ascended the Cumberland Mountain today. Road slick with rain. Doubled teams. Ruts and potholes growing worse. Once again had to pay a high and unfair toll — 73¢ a wagon and 12½¢ a horse. Some of the parties behind us may try to find a road to take them around these tollgates where greedy men are cheating us.

We made eight miles today.

October 13, 1838

Descended the mountain. Brakes failed on one wagon. It overran the horses and then tipped over. One horse was killed. One older man and one young girl with broken legs. No others hurt. Our doctor set their limbs and made them comfortable. Preacher Tsan and I were among those who righted the wagon and pulled the injured out from beneath it. Rest of column continued to move while several men stayed back to repair the wagon, which will take at least a full day. It will join one of the detachments coming on behind us. Despite the accident, we made twelve miles today and halted at the Collins River. There we made camp, issued corn and fodder and cornmeal.

October 15, 1838

Rode back and forth all day to see progress of other detachments ahead and behind. Just as in our party, they find it hard to rouse the people each morning from their blankets. It sometimes takes all of the morning to get everyone upon the trail again, moving forward in a slow shuffle. People turn and look back at our mountains with tears in their eyes. Each day at least one person does not rise from their blankets and a grave must be dug by the roadside.

In some detachments whooping cough has appeared once again among the small children. We are still suffering for the want of sufficient clothing. We have been promised that warmer clothes will be issued when we reach Nashville, where Lewis Ross has contracted for our supplies. Eighty or ninety people now on the sick list.

Trouble in Reverend Bushyhead's party with their animals. The oxen have eaten poison ivy and are sick. They have pulled over until the oxen are well again. Detachment led by Situwakee and Evan Jones has passed them.

October 19, 1838

Passed through McMinnville in early morning; watered horses and oxen at ford in river. Next water was twelve miles ahead. Made camp at Stone's River near Woodbury. Ben Rainfrog kicked by his horse while it was being reshod. Two broken ribs.

October 20, 1838

I have written nothing about my family for some time. It is because we have been blessed with as good fortune as anyone may enjoy on this sad journey. My dear mother and my two sisters are strong and well. All of them are able to walk and keep up with the wagons without any great difficulty. My mother has taken on the task of driving the oxen that pull the wagon. She strides beside them with a long whip that she cracks over their backs, popping the air but never touching the animals themselves. Emily's cough has completely vanished. Ruthie has grown an inch in height and now she is the sister who is always hungry.

I am thankful for their health and for the help our dear friend Preacher Tsan gives them almost every day.

Elizabeth remains with us also. Today she gave me a scarf to wear about my neck. I did not know what to say, but she knotted it about my neck and then looked up at me with satisfaction. Napoleyan nudged her gently with his nose as she stood beside me. She responded by stroking his cheek. He seldom favors anyone in this way, far preferring kicks and bites as a show of affection. I took it, as did Elizabeth, that my cussed mule approves her presence in our company.

October 21, 1838

Rode ahead ten miles and spent this day with Reverend Jesse Bushyhead's detachment. Oxen are recovered from the poison ivy, but their progress is still slow. They have been encamped two days now, remaining near McMinnville, Kentucky, to regain their strength. Many old and infirm in his party as well as a number of discontents who have given themselves to drink. Though there are many Christian Cherokees in his party, the great majority do not profess any Christian faith.

Shared in Reverend Bushyhead's services, which took place in the old mill at Shell's Ford on the Collins River, where he preached to a large audience. Three were baptized.

A good number of the white citizens of McMinnville took part in the services and commented on how fine a preacher Reverend Bushyhead is. There is much sympathy in this town for the Cherokees.

October 22, 1838

Reverend Bushyhead's party held a council. They were compelled to leave without satisfaction of their claims. They fear fraudulent demands will be made to defeat them. They urge that no further consideration of these demands be had while the Indians are denied the opportunity to being present or represented. I am carrying this message from them to John Ross. I will ride back with it until I meet Lew Hildebrand or another of our Nation's couriers who will carry it the rest of the way.

October 25, 1838

Rode ahead with a message for Conductor Elijah Hicks. Today was spent in the company of the Hicks party. They have experienced considerable difficulty with drunkenness. My friend Bear in the Water is with this party. When first he saw me early in the morning, he raised his hand in greeting and made no move to come closer. I know it was because he did not wish me to smell the whiskey upon his breath. My heart sank in my chest when I saw him, but I raised my hand back in greeting toward him and then I moved on to deliver my messages.

Nocowee, who had been one of the leaders of this party, has completely given himself up to whiskey. For several days the Light Horse had to drive him along the road with his hands fettered.

Chief White Path died today. His age, his sickness, and the hardships of the journey were too much for him. I watched this evening as he was buried close to the road, facing the east. Bear in the Water was one of those who helped dig the grave. He seemed sober, and there were tears in his eyes. White Path was his uncle. A tall pole painted white was erected over White Path's grave. A flag of white linen flies from its top to tell all who pass that the body of a great man rests here.

On this same day two infants were also buried.

November 5, 1838

Perhaps it is hard for you to imagine what it is like in our villages upon wheels. Here is a description of how each of our camps are set up each day.

In the morning, the first to leave are the hunters. With bows and arrows and their long blowguns (which are excellent for such small game as birds and squirrels) they fan out to either side of the route of march. Our conductor has told them where our camping place will be that night, and they will meet us there. All through the day they hunt, and when we see them again each shall have whatever game they could catch. One may bring in a brace of turkeys, another may be waiting with a fat deer. Yet another carries three squirrels, each pierced in the neck by a blowgun dart.

After the hunters, the wagons set out. The first to go is the wagon farthest along the trail, for our camps are made in a long line of lodges, each family or wagon setting up their own lodge circle. When that wagon reaches our next appointed camp, it will be the first to stop. The second wagon will go beyond it and make their halt and so on. Thus, the next morning the first to set out shall be the one that was last the day before.

At the next camp, ten miles farther down the road, the Commissary and Assistant Commissary will be waiting with wagons driven by local farmers, filled with the corn and fodder we have purchased. If we are fortunate, we shall be near a mill, and the corn will be ground. If not, then the women of each lodge will bring out their mortars, the hollowed base of a tree. Then, with wooden pestles, they will pound the corn, sieve it out, pound it again, and so on until there is enough flour for cooking.

While some prepare the corn, filling the camp with such a thumping, it is as if a hundred drums were being beaten all at once, others gather wood for fires. Men on horses, our police among them, drag in dry wood behind them with ropes fastened to their saddles as children pick up twigs and small sticks. If we are lucky, there is enough dry wood. If we are very lucky, it is not a day when it is cold or raining or snowing — though such days are precious and few. Then, when the fires are made and our lodges all set up, some with blankets or canvas tied up as lean-tos next to the wagons, there is some time for relaxation.

Then, at times, the children begin to play. They play our old game of chunky, in which spears are thrown toward a rolling target. They play stickball or shoot arrows at marks set up on tree trunks. They pass the intricately woven strings of a cat's cradle back and forth between their hands. There is a little laughter as they play, but only a little, and their play is brief, for all are exhausted after another day on the trail.

Visitors wander through our camp, stopping now and then by our fires to speak with us. Some are the tradesmen who have brought us supplies. They are often courteous to us. Some are ministers or kindly intentioned people who donate clothing or food. Others are merely curious white people who wander through looking at us as if we were forest animals dressed in clothing. Our Light Horse keep a close watch to make sure that none are selling whiskey. Sadly, at each place we stop, those who have given themselves to drink usually find some way of purchasing more.

Night falls, early and dark. Those who have come to our camp to visit must leave. We allow none but our own people to remain with us after 9 O'C P.M. The people fall into an exhausted slumber. Yet their rest is no rest from the pain they must always bear with them. To them, in their sleep come the dear faces of those who have died, those whose touch they will not know again on this side of the grave. Many cry out in the night as dreams and memories come to remind them of the pain they have endured and the trials that still lie ahead.

November 6, 1838

Crossed the Cumberland River on Nashville Toll Bridge. Two days behind Situwakee and Jones. As always, over-charged with not a thank-you from the toll collectors. Rations and supplies waiting for us in Nashville procured by Lewis Ross. Corn and fodder and oats. Also warm clothes, which will be greatly needed as the weather has quickly grown colder. Blankets, cloaks, bearskins, overcoats, thick boots, heavy socks.

Camped near Mr. Putnam's. We are not far from the Hermitage. Several men in our party also fought at Horseshoe Bend. But none rode out to make a courtesy call on Old Hickory as did a number of our people led through here by the army a year ago in October of '37. Among them were James Starr and Charles Reese, two Cherokee men who served under General Jackson in several battles during the Red Stick Rebellion. Both of them, Starr and Reese, rode out to the Hermitage to visit their old commander and were received graciously by himself and joined Old Hickory for tea.

It is said that Old Hickory is not well. When he learned that John Ross had been given the contract that we should conduct our own removal, the ex-president wrote an angry letter of protest to U.S. Attorney General Felix Grundy. "Why is it that the scamp Ross is not banished from the notice of administration?" he wrote. He urged (to no avail) that the contract be arrested. His words were totally ignored. That is one of the few things in the story of our removal that brings a smile to Cherokee faces.

November 9, 1838

Camped near Long Creek.

These are the chores that our policemen must undertake on a typical day:

> Confiscate whiskey (of which, sadly, there is always a new store to be found, sometimes hidden in such clever places as the false bottom of a trunk or tied into a sack beneath a wagon);
> & receive the food and fodder waiting at various stops and junctions;
> & find drinkable water and see to the orderly watering of teams as well as the filling of water casks;
> & order the slit trenches dug and see that the task is adequately done;
> & see to the gathering of firewood that is increasingly scarce;
> & get a few fires built and ensure that cooking is taken care of;
> & assist our doctor in identifying those who are sick and seeing that they are cared for;
> & burn the blankets of those who have contagion and died;
> & when clothing or footwear is available, distribute it

to those who are shoeless or whose clothing has worn to rags and tatters;

& patrol the camp at night to ask those who cry out to be quiet that others might sleep and see that no ill is done and that no thieves have crept in to steal from our people;

& wake the camp the next morning, though many have no wish to waken and sometimes there are those who will never wake again;

& dig graves to bury the dead;

& mound over the slit trenches with earth and bury the garbage to keep the rats and wild dogs from invading our camp;

& confiscate whiskey yet again;

& before we move on, take the roll of all to see that none are forgotten, to note those who have deserted, of which there are at least one or two each week, although there are also those who have grown confused and wandered off and become lost and so we must search for them to try to save them from harm.

I have not yet found time to speak to Reverend Foreman and ask that I might borrow a book from him. There has been, as you might imagine, little time for reading.

November 10, 1838

Passed through Port Royal, Kentucky. Excessive rain today made the travel miserable. Our fires sputter from the rain. The wind blows freezing rain in through our tents. I will cease writing now and put my journal back into my pack to protect it from this rain.

November 11, 1838

Among our party are two families of Creek Indians. The removal of the 20,000 of their nation to the western lands took place in 1836. Like others of their people, they sought refuge among the Cherokees and are counted now as Cherokee.

This evening, around the fire, I sat with one of those Creek Indians, a man of thirty-seven named Jim Tiger. He was one of the regiment of Creek warriors who fought under American officers in Florida against the Seminole while their families remained in the Creek concentration camps in Alabama.

Jim Tiger's Story

When removal came, the Creek soldiers who helped the Americans were packed onto steamboats at New Orleans along with their families and all the others and shipped west. This river travel frightened them greatly. Their fears were well founded. The boat on which Jim Tiger and six hundred others had been placed, a steamer called the *Monmouth,* was poorly captained. Late at night on the wide Mississippi, it collided with another boat and was cut in two. More than three hundred Creeks drowned, Jim Tiger's aunt among them. He and his remaining family fled back to our Cherokee Nation rather than continue that dreaded journey.

Now he found himself forced west again. "But at least," he said, "there is earth beneath our feet on this trail, not water."

November 12, 1838

On the move again after pausing yesterday for Sunday devotions. I wonder if we should also be traveling on Sundays. Our progress has been too slow, and the weather is worsening. Snow has fallen all day — wet, driving snow pushed into our faces by a cold northern wind. We are grateful for the warmer clothing provided us in Nashville, but wish there had been more. Many of us are still thinly clothed.

Reverend Foreman had a rather lengthy conversation with me yesterday after religious services. He knew some of my teachers at the Mission School and said he heard I was a promising scholar. I replied that my Latin was good but that I have only small knowledge of Greek, and almost none at all of Hebrew. I confessed that though I had owned a small library — now sadly lost to me — I had little knowledge of the classics and had read through the Bible from cover to cover no more than six times at most. For some reason he smiled at that.

He urged that I should continue my studies in the west. There, he promised, we will soon have schools set up, including seminaries for both girls and boys. Though we have lost our homeland, we have not lost our spirit. We shall remain Cherokee and rise again. *"Nova ex veteris,"* he concluded.

I nodded my head. "The new must come out of the old."

Reverend Foreman appeared to approve my weak translation of his Latin.

"Not only students will be needed, but also those of our people educated enough to become teachers," he said, his hand upon my shoulder.

Then, even before I asked, he offered to lend me one of his books. Imagine my surprise when the volume he chose to hand to me was the very one I had begun to read but never finished. It was my old friend and fellow castaway Robinson Crusoe!

I have read twenty more pages of it this evening! My sad surroundings quite faded away as I became lost in the story. I must confess, however, that it seems to me the good man Friday might be a Cherokee, a younger version of the Feeler. Also I find myself picturing the cannibals in the story as members of the Georgia Guard!

November 13, 1838

This morning, as I went to the water, I felt I was not alone. I looked up from the flowing stream after having washed my forehead. To my surprise I saw the Feeler standing on the other side, downstream from me. He stared at me so intently that it seemed as if he were looking through me. I made as if to cross over to him. He held up his right hand, motioning me to stay where I was.

"Grandfather," I said to him, "are you coming with us to the west?"

He smiled and went down on one knee to put his hands upon the soil. I understood. He was staying in our old land.

He stood up again. I saw he was no longer carrying his book in the pack that had always been slung over his shoulder. Was his book what he had placed in the hollow tree in my dream? I suddenly realized the Feeler's motions were less stiff than the last time I saw him. He no longer used a staff. My great-great-grandfather placed his hand on his heart and then swung it out, palm opened, toward me. I did the same in return. My eyes filled with tears as I did so. His image blurred in my sight, and then, like mist blown away by the wind, he was gone.

I know that I shall never see him again in this lifetime.

November 14, 1838

We are camped near Hopkinsville, Kentucky. Several parties have already passed through here before us and they have excited the pity of the local townsfolk. Their newspaper, the *Hopkinsville Gazette,* contained an article urging the good people of the town to help us. Though we had been driven from our homes by whites, we found the white people here sympathetic with our distress. They have brought food and clothing to our encampment and made generous donations for our comfort.

November 16, 1838

One child died today of whooping cough. Her smallness made the burial easier, for it was not so hard to find the boards for the coffin or to dig the hole.

Sat again with Jim Tiger. I spoke with him of how hard it was to see the sickness among our people.

"At least," he said, "it is not smallpox." Then he related another tale of the removal of his Creek people.

Jim Tiger's Second Story

A friend of Jim Tiger's who went by the name of Talledega Joe told him this story. Talledega Joe was also making his way back from the west to hide among the Cherokee. It was late December and it was very cold and he had lost the trail. Then, at midday, Talledega Joe saw a cabin on a hilltop with a wisp of smoke coming from the chimney. Though it was far away from him, Talledega Joe, who was blessed with great eyesight, could make out the figure of a thin, stooped Indian man with a blanket about his shoulders, sitting on the gallery porch.

But as Talledega Joe started up the hill toward that cabin, the man who sat there saw him. That man stood shakily and waved at him to stop. The man, who was dressed in Creek fashion, pointed with his hand to a roughly fashioned flag that flew above the cabin. It was white with red spots painted upon it. Then the man made signs indicating that he was not alone, that sick people were inside the cabin.

Talledega Joe understood. The flag meant smallpox was there. That Creek man was one of a party of scouts who had stumbled upon the cabin and found that the people within had that awful disease.

They knew, as do all of our Indian people, that to return to their people would mean they would bring the terrible sickness — for which we have no cure — back among them. So the Creek scouts decided to stay in that cabin and wait for death. They had raised that warning flag and were keeping watch to warn others away.

His eyes moist, Talledega Joe turned his face away from that hilltop of self-sacrifice and continued on. When he had climbed another hill he looked back across the valley and saw a pillar of smoke rising. Rather than take a chance that someone else might come upon them and not be warned away soon enough, the dying Creek scouts had set fire to their cabin.

November 17, 1838

We have passed Salem, Kentucky, and are approaching the Ohio River. There we shall cross over by flatboats to Golconda, Illinois. The weather is very cold. Ice has formed in our water kegs each morning. It seems that the rivers will freeze early. Some worry we will be caught between the two rivers we must cross — the Ohio and the Mississippi. If there is floating ice, the ferries cannot run. We will then be forced to make camp until the ice clears from the river. I pray this will not happen, but the progress of our long line of detachments has been painful and slow.

This morning, before sunrise, I went to the water, a creek that is said to flow down to the Ohio. I spoke to the old Long Man in Cherokee as the Feeler taught me. I asked that the Ohio take pity upon our people and that we be allowed to cross over.

This was not, I think, a bad thing to do. Did not Moses himself ask that the waters of the Red Sea be parted to allow the Israelites to pass to the other side? Still, I did not tell Reverend Foreman of my actions.

When I came walking up from the stream I found Elizabeth at the top of the bank. The sun was rising behind her. She took me by the hand, and we walked together without speaking back to the wagon where my mother and my sisters had already harnessed up the team.

With the cold weather, even more people are becoming ill. Never enough blankets. Never enough fuel for the fires, and the detachments behind will find even less after we pass.

November 19, 1838

Broke camp at 7 O'C A.M. At 10 O'C A.M. arrived at Berry's Ferry. Ice at the river's edge, but the flatboat ferry was running. The wind was calm, and the river was not at all rough. Our crossing was a smooth one, though many of the people were very afraid while out on the broad river. All wagons had been taken over by 6 O'C P.M.

We moved on an hour farther beyond the river to make our camp for the night. It has been decided we will make camp for several days here. Everyone in our party is too exhausted to press on quickly. The three detachments ahead of us have sent word back that they expect to cross the Mississippi within the next few days.

We will also wait to see how the Bushyhead group fares in crossing the Ohio. We passed them by on the road three days before our own crossing.

November 21, 1838

Snow upon the ground. Reverend Bushyhead's party took two days to cross the Ohio, but it is now on its way, about ten miles behind us. We are also on our way again. It is our hope that the Mississippi will allow us to pass over its dangerous waters without incident. But the other couriers tell me that there is ice upon the Great River and the weather has grown ever colder.

November 25, 1838

We are camped southeast of Vienna, Illinois. It is again Sunday, and so we are not traveling. The three parties ahead of us have crossed the Mississippi, a perilous crossing with ice floating in the river. There are still eight detachments behind us. The last of our parties to take this route by land is the one led by Richard Taylor and Daniel Butrick. They departed only three weeks ago.

Our faithful chief, John Ross, like the captain who will not leave the bridge of his ship until the last are in the lifeboats, still remains in the Nation. He is packing up the papers of our Nation. He will engage a steamer to take him and his family, along with those few remaining Cherokees who are too infirm or ill to go by land. They will go by the river route to Little Rock.

December 2, 1838

Our progress is agonizingly slow across the narrow neck of Illinois between the rivers. To the east and south of us is the Ohio, which is joined by the Tennessee before the two rivers flow into the Mississippi. There is no way out of this arc of land except to cross the river.

Once again we are stopped and shall not travel because it is Sunday. But it seems that hurrying now will be of no avail. I scouted ahead today with our Light Horse and saw the Mississippi River. Great blocks of ice are flowing down. The Great River is growling like some huge and hungry beast as the ice scrapes the shore. Three of our parties have crossed, but it seems that we shall not. The ferries are not running. We are trapped.

December 4, 1838

There are two ferry crossings. The northern one is to Cape Girardeau, Missouri. The second crossing is at Green's Ferry. Both are closed and will remain so until there is a thaw.

We are now all encamped and will remain so until the Mississippi sees fit to allow us upon her. It is very cold. Much snow. Many are becoming ill in all seven of our detachments held here by the ice. Five died on our way to this encampment, and it was hard to dig the graves in the frozen earth. We finally covered the shallow burials with logs and stones.

My mother has visited the Bushyhead encampment to see her good friend Nanny, Reverend Bushyhead's sister. She is concerned. Nanny has a persistent cough and is quite weak.

Reverend Bushyhead's wife is growing near her time and will probably give birth near the end of this month.

December 6, 1838

Rode out again to look at the Mississippi. As I sat on a bluff, a white bird flew overhead, heading west. The Great River is no barrier to the flight of birds. They leave their homes and return again each year. But we Cherokees have no wings. So we must suffer upon the ground when we are thrown from our nests.

December 9, 1838

Two were baptized by Reverend Bushyhead today in a small river that flows into the Mississippi.

Three died yesterday. One was the girl baby born last night to Jane Nakee, wife of Long Wind. One was Nick, a black slave. One was Mary Welch, the white wife of John Welch, a formerly prosperous Cherokee plantation owner. The Welchs had been married for nineteen years.

December 12, 1838

The ice still chokes the Great River. Snow falling again. Many are sick from sleeping upon the frozen ground.

December 16, 1838

Assisted John Iron with blacksmithing. Many of the horses and mules need to be reshod. There was also repair to be made on metal parts of wagons. Blacksmithing is one of those things I have often been curious about, and he was willing enough to teach me.

At the end of the day John Iron said I would make a

good smith, for I am strong and my eyes are keen and the fire does not seem to frighten me as it does many.

December 25, 1838

Christmas celebrated by the Christians among us. Few gifts to exchange other than wishes for health and good fortune. The singing of Christmas songs in Cherokee was quite beautiful, and even the weak among us seemed to grow stronger as the singing continued.

One child born this day to Culasuttee's family in Jesse Bushyhead's Baptist congregation. They named him Samuel. No wise men came to see him.

January 1, 1839

I pick up this journal again after having had little to say and even less time to write for the last few days. Our camps have not been able to move, strung out across the face of southern Illinois like drops of water frozen on a window.

But because we have not been able to move, because of the snow and the cold, because of the sickness and the dying, because of the scarcity of firewood, all of us who were able-bodied have been kept busy each day. Many days have been spent riding for miles to find dry wood and then load it into wagons or drag it back to camp behind our horses and mules. Ancient Red has never been more needed by our people, for the tents and blankets are too thin to keep out the wintry blasts. We have had many funerals, far too many. I have stopped keeping count. Our hands, which once were blistered from the shovels, have now grown thickly calloused from the digging of so many graves.

I have also been kept busy as a courier and also in scouting for supplies that we may purchase. The cold weather seems to bother my mule Napoleyan not one whit, and he is tireless even as we go through deep snow and have to ride far. The closest farms have run out of grain and corn to sell us. To their everlasting credit, these white farmers of Illinois have charged us no more than the fair market price for their corn and fodder. But they have no more. So we have had to range farther to supply food for our people and our animals.

Our hunters have also emptied the nearby forests of game. Some travel for two or three days to the north just to bring back a single deer. We have purchased some cattle and a few pigs from farmers. We also have purchased bacon and salt pork. All of us exist now on much less food than at any time in our journey. Many are suffering from the flux.

Today the weather began to change. I felt a warmer

breeze. When we rode to the Great River and looked out, we saw that the ice was clearing from its moody face. There are no new floes in sight coming down the river. The ferrymen say they will risk a crossing tomorrow.

January 4, 1839

Jackson, Missouri. We are in camp here. Our crossing took two full days. Reverend Bushyhead was set to cross behind us, but we did not wait for his party. Instead, we moved on as quickly as possible. Our hunters left a space of twelve miles behind us in which the later groups might find game.

January 5, 1839

My mother received a message from Reverend Bushyhead. His beloved sister, her dear friend Nanny, died on January 4 after crossing over the Mississippi. During that same crossing, Reverend Bushyhead's wife gave birth to a daughter. They named her Eliza Missouri.

Nova ex veteris.

January 8, 1839

I have mentioned the blacks among us who are slaves. Often their masters treat them much like family members, although when it comes time for gathering wood or making the meals, it is usually the blacks who do it.

One is a young woman named Flora. She has been a friend to my two little sisters. When she was not working, she spent time playing and talking with them. Today we bade her farewell. But it was not a sad farewell. A white man who visited our camp on his way back home to the south recognized her. She had been sold from the plantation of his father to a wealthy Cherokee man some eight or nine years ago. He informed her that her family was still alive and well, including her parents. If she wished to return home, he told her, he would purchase her from her Cherokee master. She was eager and excited to do so, and her owner was agreeable.

Before she left, she reached into her apron and took out a packet. It contained hollyhock seeds she had gathered from flowers grown in the earth of our lost Cherokee Nation. She gave each of my sisters a small handful of those seeds, urging them to plant them in their new home in the west. That way she and the memory of our land would be with us each spring.

January 13, 1839

We have passed Little Prairie.

Chief Ross called a meeting for the conductors of all

of the parties on this side of the Mississippi River. He urged them to speed their journey by traveling at least half of the day on Sundays when all in their parties are well and strong enough to do so. All of our detachments have lost many days of travel when they have had to remain in camp because of illness.

Meanwhile, word comes to us that the Elijah Hicks party has already reached the western lands on the 4th or 5th of January. Their journey is done, but ours still has weeks to go, for more than 250 miles yet lay ahead of us.

Though it is a Sunday, we traveled half of the day and made six miles before camping.

January 14, 1839

Missouri seems much less peopled than any of the other states through which we passed. Farms are few, and the towns are much smaller. It is not always easy to get corn for our food or fodder for our animals. Still, the farmers and merchants treat us fairly. Our only continuing problem with the white people remains the whiskey sellers. They are like buzzards, constantly circling and looking for the weakest upon whom they may prey.

January 15, 1839

The weather continues to change from one day to the next. Today it is quite sunny, and the snow is melting away. Yesterday we drove into blizzards of sleet and snow. Tomorrow it will surely snow again.

January 18, 1839

A difficult day today. At dawn we discovered that several men were missing. Snail, Matthew Crane, Isaac Helter. Their families were concerned, for all three had been drinking. Arrow Toter and two other Light Horse and I followed their tracks through the snow. It was easy to do, for all were barefoot, and after a mile or so their tracks were marked by blood from their feet being cut by the snow crust. We found Snail first, unconscious. One of the men threw him over his horse like a sack of potatoes to take him back to the camp to thaw him and sober him.

Isaac Helter and Matthew Crane were more difficult. We found them at the mouth of a cave, hurling stones into it. They had armed themselves with clubs and fought us, shouting as they did so. All of us were bruised. We had to rope both men and tie them to bring them back. Helter kept raving in his drunkenness that they had planned to catch Major Ridge and kill him as a traitor. He was quite convinced that Major Ridge had taken shelter from them inside that cave.

It saddened me greatly. Helter, in particular, has been a good man throughout the journey. He had a small farm not far from our own. He has always been quiet and helpful to others. I think the death of his wife to ague last week is the cause of his drinking. I am afraid that now he has begun to drink, he will continue to do so. I have seen this happen to many others along our way.

I vow that I shall never drink.

JANUARY 20, 1839

I dreamed last night of the Feeler. We stood together in the forest. We had just gone to the water together. He held tobacco in his hand and then placed it into a pouch, which he handed to me. Then he put his hand upon the trunk of a hollow tree. It was the same tree in which I concealed my father's musket.

"It is waiting for you in here," he said in Cherokee. I knew that he did not mean the gun. I knew he meant his book in which all of his formulas were written.

Soon after dawn, after breaking camp, Tsan came to me. He held a pouch that looked familiar in his hand. "This pouch, I thought I had lost it," he said. "But it was only hiding from me at the bottom of my saddlebags.

When I last saw him two months ago, your old grandfather asked me to give it to you."

January 24, 1839

We camped last night at the James fork of the White River, which flows beside the road here. Springfield is a three-day journey ahead of us. The river here is well suited for baptism. I am sure that Reverend Bushyhead will make use of it when his party reaches here. They are now five or six days behind us.

I went down to the river before dawn, taking some of the tobacco from the pouch given to me by the Feeler. I prayed for the safety of my family, all of those in our care.

January 27, 1839

Started out at 9 O'C A.M. and passed through Springfield. Halted and encamped at 5 O'C P.M. Eleven miles today without incident. No deaths this past week. No desertions, no incidents of drunkenness.

February 1, 1839

Pushing on through Missouri at a slow but steady pace. Warmer weather today. Ground is bare of snow in many places as we pass.

With so few unfortunate incidents, there has been more time to think. As I ride along on the back of my red mule I wonder what path I shall pursue in my new life. Of course I will help my mother and my sisters to build a new home. Since I am the only man in our family, that may prevent me from leaving to do other things for some years. But if I were free to leave, what would I do?

I have found the life of a Light Horse policeman interesting, though I confess I do not like the rough way we must sometimes treat others, especially those who are drunk. I also do not like the fact that we are sometimes charged with bringing back slaves who have run away — as has happened three times on this journey.

I was told by John Iron I could make a good blacksmith. As a blacksmith I would always have work to do.

I also think of the Feeler's book, which waits for me in that hollow tree in our old lands. Someday I shall return for the gun and the book. But what shall I then do with them?

I could become a scholar. I could become learned and write and translate, as did John Brown. Or I could help in the rebirth of a newspaper for our Nation in the west and write for it as did E. B. for the *Cherokee Phoenix*.

Whatever path is open to me, I shall have some money of my own to spend upon it. Though I plan to give half of the wages I have earned for my work on this journey to my mother and sisters, I shall keep half for myself. It may amount to as much as thirty dollars, a large sum indeed.

February 4, 1839

I should not have said that all was peaceful. The day before yesterday two teams ran away as they were being hitched. One of our hunters shot another with an arrow by accident (though the wound was only in his arm). A horse stepped into a woodchuck hole, broke its leg, and had to be shot, and a band of five young men became drunk and kept the camp awake late at night singing songs until we were compelled to bind and gag them.

I was kept busy not only with all of those incidents that I witnessed or was involved in, but also had to carry a message to the detachment before us one day and the one behind the next. Just writing about all this makes me feel tired.

With all that, our party was compelled to spend two days in camp and made no progress west.

February 6, 1839

Rain fell this morning, snow by afternoon. Road treacherous.

February 8, 1839

Hunting is very poor. Hunters brought in only fourteen deer, ten turkeys, and six dozen squirrels. Little enough for our party of over nine hundred. Later detachments may have to take alternate roads. We have swept this land clean of game.

February 10, 1839

Received a great shock today. My mother and my friend Preacher Tsan came to me and told me they are to be married. I knew they spent time together in my absence, but I did not know they had grown close in this way. It is true that my two sisters already treat Tsan as if he were a well-loved uncle and that they would certainly welcome him as a permanent member of our household. It is also true that my mother is in good health and has a strong spirit, but I never thought that someone as old as she would marry again. She is thirty-six years old, which is a year or more older than Tsan himself.

Tsan further told me that she was the one who asked him to marry her and that he agreed immediately, as would any Cherokee man with sense enough to recognize a great blessing.

"Do you accept me into your mother's family, Jesse?" Tsan said to me. His voice was filled with concern. The shock of their announcement must have shown itself on my face.

In answer I threw my arms around him and hugged him so hard that he had to beg me to stop for fear I would break his spine. Though the two of them seem to me to be almost too old for marriage, I am very happy for them.

February 12, 1839

We have almost crossed Missouri and will soon pass down into Arkansas. We shall pass north and west of the lands that belonged to the western Cherokees from 1810 to 1828, before they were told they must remove beyond the borders of that state.

February 17, 1839

Reached Cane Hill, Arkansas.

February 19, 1839

Though I may wonder about my own destiny, I have now discovered that others have quite firm ideas about my future.

Reverend Foreman had a serious talk with me today. He urged me to go back to school and become a teacher. Perhaps I may do so. I told Elizabeth about my talk. She agreed that Reverend Foreman was right.

"I shall return to school, also," she said. "When we are married, we can both be teachers." She then kissed me upon the cheek and walked away.

I stood there with my hands upon my hips. Until then, I had not known that we had such marriage plans. But learning of them has not displeased me.

February 22, 1839

We are at our last camp. Tomorrow we shall end our journey. So I take up my pen today to write of a concern I have begun to feel more strongly.

Now that it seems our long journey shall indeed have an end, I wonder what awaits us in the western lands. The Cherokees who emigrated there many years before our Removal have for two decades or more enjoyed their own government. They have their own chiefs. Though our number is three times as great as theirs, I wonder if they will accept the government we bring with us.

Then there are those Cherokees who signed the fraudulent Treaty of New Echota and emigrated of their own accord. They have no love for John Ross and will fight him at every turn, especially such stubborn men as the Ridges and Stand Watie.

Most of all I worry about those among us whose hatred has grown deeper with every death along this road where our people wept and suffered. Nunda'utsun'yi is what many are now calling it. "The Trail of Tears." These angry men speak around the fires at night about the law that calls for the death of any who sell our land. They mention the names of those who signed the treaty and then spit upon the earth. They resolve that there will be a reckoning to come.

I wonder if we will pass from one trail of suffering where our people die of cold and sickness to another where we die at each other's hands?

I have made my own resolution. I will cast anger and hatred out of my heart. Though I cannot forget what they did, I shall forgive those who betrayed us. Though their actions were wrong, I shall try to believe that they did what they did because they felt there was no other way to help our people. When I see Elias Boudinot, I shall offer him my hand. If we must build a new Nation in the west, we must do it together. Our Cherokee phoenix shall rise again.

Epilogue

Jesse Smoke and his mother, Sallie, with the help of Preacher Tsan, built a small house near Park Hill, Oklahoma, at the edge of the new Cherokee capital of Tahlequah. Sallie Littledeer and Preacher Tsan were among the first Cherokee couples to be married after the Trail of Tears, and had three children, two girls and a boy. Tsan gave up circuit riding to became a deacon in the church and a part-time preacher. Together, he and Sallie ran a successful dry-goods store in Tahlequah. Aside from the time of turmoil during the Civil War, they enjoyed a long and quiet life together, celebrating their fiftieth wedding anniversary in 1889.

In the "Golden Age" of the western Cherokee Nation between 1839 and 1861, Jesse Smoke and his two sisters continued their education in Tahlequah. Jesse attended and then taught at the Male Seminary. Jesse indeed married Elizabeth — proving once again that when a Cherokee woman makes up her mind, nothing can stand in her way. Their wedding did not take place, however, until Jesse had finally made a journey back to the lands of the old Cherokee Nation in Georgia and Tennessee in the summer of 1843. Two years before, Jesse had joined the Masons, and was warmly welcomed into the homes of brother Masons as he traveled. When Jesse returned to Tahlequah, he brought with him his grandfather's gun and a package the size of a book wrapped in leather. Though few spoke of it openly to outsiders, in his later years Jesse was known as both an educator and a traditional healer.

Both of Jesse's sisters showed themselves to be as intelligent and resourceful as their mother. After finishing seminary, Ruthie started a dress shop and also hosted regular meetings of a Tahlequah Cherokee Women's Improvement Society, at which, among other things they would discuss books and plan how to better their community. In 1847, Ruthie married one of Jesse's old ball-playing friends, Snake Killer. They had four children, two boys and two girls.

Emily turned out to be a talented writer and public speaker. The American Mission Board brought her first to Boston, and then, in the years that followed, sent her on speaking tours to England and Europe. She became fluent in French and Spanish. While in Washington, D.C., she met a young man, Thomas Blacksnake, from the Seneca Nation in New York State, who was in the capital with a delegation from his people regarding land claims. The two began to correspond, and married in 1850. The home they built together on the Cattaraugus Seneca Reservation became a place of refuge for the rest of Jesse's family during the terrible days of the Civil War. Jesse's mother, Preacher Tsan, Ruthie, and her two daughters spent two years at the Blacksnake home in New York until the war was over. Jesse himself traveled to Washington as part of delegations led by John Ross on several occasions during and after the war. However, unlike many pro-Ross Cherokees, he did not serve in the Union army. After seeing the terrible events of 1839, Jesse vowed that he would never shed the blood of another Cherokee, and he kept that vow all his life.

Napoleyan, Jesse's cussed stubborn mule, lived to the age of twenty-eight. Napoleyan's last act was to kick the veterinarian who was trying to tend him, breaking two of the man's ribs. The old red mule then expired with what Jesse swore was a smile on his face.

White Will, Jesse's friend from the camps, devoted several more years of his life to the military. Inspired by his brief friendship with Jesse, he learned to read and write, and rose eventually to the rank of sergeant. After his military service ended, Will took a job at the Qualla Principal Trading Store in North Carolina, next to what finally became the Eastern Cherokee Reservation. In 1843,

Will married a Cherokee woman named Betsy Fence Maker. Adopted by her family, Will learned to speak Cherokee and lived among the Cherokees, urging their seven children to always respect both the Indian and the white sides of their families. He went on to work for the Western North Carolina Railroad and was quite prosperous at the time when the Civil War broke out in 1861. During the war, Will enlisted in the Thomas Legion, which included four companies of Cherokees who had all volunteered for the South. The Thomas Legion saw little action, mostly serving as a border guard for the Confederacy along the mountain region. Will escaped the war unscathed and lived to the age of seventy-three.

After the Civil War, Tahlequah was rebuilt. Once again, Jesse and his family enjoyed many years of peace.

What finally happened to Jesse Smoke? No one knows for certain. After the death of his wife, Elizabeth, from influenza in the winter of 1898, Jesse told his 7 children, 36 grandchildren, and 110 great-grandchildren that the time had come for him to finally go home and climb one last mountain. He bought a train ticket east. The last his family heard of him was a letter sent to them from Nashville, Tennessee, dated July 7, 1899. "Visited the grave of Andrew Jackson," it read. "I am pleased to report he is still dead." Nothing further was ever heard from Jesse.

However, his great-granddaughter, Amelia Smoke Starr,

who inherited his journal, says that she has heard a story from the North Carolina Cherokees about an elderly Cherokee man in very good health who turned up in Cherokee, North Carolina, about that time. The man, who was tall and strong despite his age, knew a good deal about the old healing ways and said only that his name was Gogisgi. That man may not have been Jesse, since it is reported that he lived there for fifty more years — which would have made him over 130 years of age. Gogisgi's death was not recorded. He simple vanished one day into the woods, following the tracks of a bear up toward Clingman's Dome.

Life in America in 1837

Historical Note

In 1817, President James Monroe made a promise to the Cherokees, the largest tribe east of the Mississippi River. "As long as water flows," Monroe said, "or grass grows upon the earth, or the sun rises to show your pathway, or you kindle your camp fires, so long shall you be protected by this Government, and never again removed from your present habitations."

Despite that solemn promise, only thirteen years later, Indian Removal to the western territories was in full force. The Seminoles of Florida resisted by waging guerrilla warfare. Others, including several thousand Cherokees, moved peaceably, feeling they had no choice. The bulk of the Cherokee Nation, united behind the leadership of John Ross, carried their case into the courts, as far as the U.S. Supreme Court, where a historic judgment was made favoring the Cherokees. In the end, however, the vast majority of American Indians were removed from the southeast. In addition to the 17,000 Cherokees, as many as 65,000 other Indians were forced to leave. They were sent west on the bitter road the Cherokees call Nunda'utsun'yi, "the Place Where the People Cried," or "the Trail of Tears." Today the tearing of nations from their homelands would be called ethnic cleansing, a crime against humanity. In 1830 it was called Indian Removal.

What led to this? Why did the United States break its word with these Native nations? To understand, we must look back in history.

The Cherokees, by the nineteenth century, had long been acquainted with white men. Their first European contact was in 1540 with the Spanish explorer Hernando DeSoto, who found the Cherokee living in large, well-organized towns. They called themselves Ani-yonega, "the Principal People." Cherokee, the name Europeans gave them, probably comes from the Creek word jilagi, which means, "Those of a Different Speech." The Cherokees, respected as the largest and most powerful of the southern tribes, controlled much of present-day Tennessee, Georgia, Kentucky, northeastern Alabama, western North Carolina, South Carolina, West Virginia, and Virginia. Europeans settled around their lands and traded with them.

The growth of English settlements eventually brought them into conflict with the Cherokees, who kept out most white settlers until the mid-1750s. The French and Indian War, from 1756 to 1763, deeply impacted the Cherokees. At first, they supported the English against the French. Then the murder of several Cherokee chiefs by the English led to a war with the British. Cherokee towns in South Carolina, Tennessee, and Georgia were wiped out. At least 5,000 Cherokees died. Much of their territory was ceded to the English. By 1775, the Cherokees had lost all of Virginia, West Virginia, and Kentucky.

During the American Revolution, most Cherokees sided with the British. Fifty Cherokee towns were destroyed, and more land was taken. In October 1794, the Peace Treaty of Tellico Blockhouse, signed by Chief Bloody Fellow, ended all warfare between the Cherokees and the United States. Cherokee lands were less than one quarter their former size.

During the War of 1812, many Cherokees fought on the side of the United States against the British. In 1814, Cherokee volunteers led by General Andrew Jackson were the deciding factor in the Battle of Horseshoe Bend against the Red Stick Creeks, saving Jackson's army and reputation. Among the Cherokee fighters were three men whose names would become famous: Sequoyah, John Ross, and Major Ridge.

By 1800, two choices lay before the Cherokees. One was to migrate west. Some favored that choice and moved to Missouri. The second option was to remain Indian at heart and maintain tribal governments and languages, but outwardly adopt European culture. The Cherokees and their neighbors did this so well that they became known as "the Five Civilized Tribes." Their clothing, their homes and plantations, and even the ability of many Indians to speak and write in English matched their white neighbors. Because many whites had been adopted and married Cherokees, some "mixed-blood" Cherokees were now physically indistinguishable from non-Indians. Wealthier Cherokees even owned African slaves to work their large plantations. The Cherokee Nation changed its government from loosely allied towns to a National Council with eight electoral districts. New Echota in Georgia became the capital of the Cherokee Nation.

In 1821, Sequoyah, after twenty-two years of work, presented to the Council a syllabary, an alphabet of eighty-six symbols. Cherokees quickly learned to read and write their own language. By 1828, they had their own printing press and were publishing books and their own newspaper, the *Cherokee Phoenix*, in English and in Cherokee. In 1822, a Cherokee Supreme Court was established. In 1827, the Cherokees adopted a constitution modeled on that of the United States Constitution. John Ross, a brilliant politician deeply loyal to his people, though only one-eighth Cherokee, was elected Principal Chief.

Despite their advances in civilization, powerful forces still opposed the Cherokees. The loudest voice demanding Cherokee Removal was the state of Georgia. In 1802, Georgia gave up its western territories (which became Alabama) in exchange for the promise that all Indians in Georgia would be removed. After gold was discovered on Cherokee lands in Georgia in 1829, Georgia threatened to secede from the Union if the Indians were not removed.

Another powerful enemy of the Cherokees was the very general under whom they had served in 1814. In 1828, Andrew Jackson was elected president of the United States on a platform of Indian Removal. In 1830, Jackson's Indian Removal Bill was passed by one vote in Congress.

Cherokee Removal divided opinion in the United States. Many spoke against it, including former President John Quincy Adams. The Cherokees themselves had made a law that any Cherokee selling land would be punished by death. In 1807, Chief Doublehead was executed for leasing land to white settlers. Led by John Ross, the Cherokees refused to accept a cash settlement for their land or agree to their removal. Such Christian ministers as Evan Jones, Daniel Butrick, Elizur Butler, and Samuel A. Worcester, who had established Cherokee Mission Schools, campaigned on behalf of their Indian friends. The Cherokees stayed on their own lands for another eight years, the last of the southeastern tribes to remain.

Two voices against Removal were Major Ridge and a Cherokee once known as Gallegina Watie, who changed his name to Elias Boudinot to honor a New England theologian. Major Ridge, the old warrior of Horseshoe Bend, was among those who executed Chief Doublehead. Elias Boudinot had spent many years in Mission Schools in New England. As editor of the *Cherokee Phoenix*, he wrote ringing editorials defending Cherokee sovereignty.

Then, on December 29, 1835, a tragic event occurred. Though not legally empowered, Major Ridge, Elias Boudinot, and eighteen other Cherokee men signed a paper agreeing to Cherokee Removal — the infamous Treaty of New Echota. Some said they were bribed. Others say they saw no hope of getting a better deal. John Ross and the elected representatives were too stubborn to give in. Someone had to act for the good of the people. Whatever their reasons, these twenty had no right to do what they did. The result was the Trail of Tears.

The Cherokees and their many friends protested. They presented a petition signed by 15,665 Cherokees opposing the Treaty of New Echota. General John E. Wool, assigned to supervise Cherokee Removal, was so disturbed by the injustice that he resigned his commission in 1837.

General Winfield Scott, the man who followed Wool, admired the Cherokees but followed his orders. The final roundup of those who refused removal came on May 26, 1838, when 7,380 troops swept out of the night to roust the Cherokees from their homes. There was little resistance. Within three weeks, 15,000 Cherokees were crowded into thirty-one stockades in Georgia, Tennessee, Alabama, and North Carolina. From there they were concentrated into eleven concentration camps in Alabama and Tennessee. Conditions in these camps were terrible. Inadequate sanitation, poor shelter, meager food, and ill-treatment took their toll. Thousands died there.

Not only Cherokees were imprisoned. The camps also held white men and women married to Cherokees and any African-American slaves held by the Indians. The Cherokees, represented eloquently by John Ross, petitioned General Scott to delay removal until the fall. There was a terrible drought that spring and summer. Three parties sent west in June by boat had great difficulty. The rivers were too low for boats to pass. There was no drinking water along the route. Many became sick and died.

Scott agreed to suspend emigrations until fall. Then he did something that raised a howl of protest from former President Jackson. General Scott gave the Cherokees permission to direct their own Removal. Funds were allotted from the reimbursement monies provided in the Treaty of New Echota. Lewis Ross, John Ross's brother, bought horses and wagons and provided supplies at depots along the way. On August 23, 1838, the first of thirteen Cherokee detachments set out. They traveled north through Tennessee and Kentucky, crossed the Ohio River into Illinois, ferried the Mississippi River into Missouri, then passed through Arkansas to Fort Gibson, in present-day northeastern Oklahoma. The distance, depending on the route, was between 800 and 1,200 miles. It had been estimated to take only eighty days.

But heavy rains and a hard winter came early. Roads were muddy; people were weakened from the camps. In some detachments the Christian ministers, including such Cherokees as Reverend Jesse Bushyhead, refused to allow their parties to travel on Sunday. The Ohio and Mississippi filled with ice floes. Ferries could not cross. After almost four months, the first detachment reached Fort Gibson on January 4. The last arrived on March 24.

No one knows how many perished during the journey. Official records list 447 deaths. Everyone agrees that is a very low figure. Many perished while being captured and in the camps — perhaps 2,000 or more. About 800 Cherokees, weakened by their trials, died soon after reaching the west. At least 4,000 Cherokees (and perhaps twice that many) died between 1838 and 1839 as a result of the Trail of Tears — one quarter of their nation.

The first year in the new Cherokee Nation was one of rapid rebuilding. Reverend Jesse Bushyhead put up his church by using the beams brought all the way from Georgia and Tennessee. That church still stands to this day, a few miles outside of the present town of Westville, Oklahoma. The sign above the door reads "Old Baptist Mission Church, Brought from Georgia on the Trail of Tears in 1838."

The site for a new capital was chosen. Two commissioners of the Cherokee Nation met beneath a huge elm tree and declared, "Tah-le-quah," meaning "This Place Will Do." To this day, Tahlequah remains the capital of the Western Cherokee Nation.

Things were not easy. The "Old Settlers," about 4,000 Cherokees, had been there for years with their own government. The "Treaty Party" Cherokees were at odds with the "Ross Party." Although John Ross urged his people to not carry out the death penalty for selling Cherokee land (added to their written laws in 1829), a secret meeting with representatives of all seven Cherokee clans was held behind Ross's back. On July 22, 1839, assassins sought out the principal signers of the Treaty of New Echota. Major Ridge and his son John Ridge were the first to be killed. Then, Elias Boudinot, who had been placed in charge of dispensing medicines for the Cherokee Nation, was approached by two men, asking for medicine. As he turned to walk to the Mission station, one stabbed him with a knife, and the other struck him in the head with a tomahawk. Reverend Worcester and Elias Boudinot's wife, Delight, heard his cries for help but arrived too late. Worcester immediately sent a rider to the home of Boudinot's brother, Stand Watie, to warn him. To the later sorrow of the Cherokee Nation, Stand Watie escaped his assassins.

Other deaths followed. Eventually, peace was restored. One of those who spoke for reunification was Sequoyah, who had moved west in 1824. A new Cherokee government was accepted with John Ross as Principal Chief. Tahlequah became a place of commerce and culture, with schools, stores, a courthouse, and seminaries for Cherokee men and women. The Cherokee Nation enjoyed three decades of peace and prosperity before the Civil War again split their nation into two warring camps. John Ross and his supporters eventually declared for the Union. Stand Watie became a Confederate general, and his troops burned Tahlequah to the ground.

On August 1, 1866, Chief John Ross died in Washington. The Civil War was over. He was seventy-five years old and in failing health, yet he had been trying to negotiate a treaty to keep the Cherokee Nation intact. Though he did not live to see it, Ross's final efforts were not in vain: the Western Cherokee Nation remained united.

Not all Cherokees were taken west. In North Carolina, around 1,000 "citizen Cherokees" were allowed to remain.

Refugees from other parts of the southeast joined them at what would eventually become the Eastern Cherokee Reservation in Cherokee, North Carolina. Today the Eastern Cherokees and Western Cherokees communicate regularly with each other, sharing pride in their common survival. The 208,000 people of the Western Cherokee Nation are the second largest Indian tribe in the United States.

The uniqueness and spirit of Cherokee culture was evident in their daily life. A game akin to lacrosse was fiercely played. However, this was not all in the name of sport and vanity. It was a sacred ritual, a reenactment of the constant struggle between opposing forces of the universe. Here, a team gets ready for competition. The seven women, representing the seven Cherokee clans, chant to the beat of the seated drummer while the players circle a sacred fire.

The Cherokees faced many conflicts dating back to the first European contact, not the least of which came in the early 1800s when they chose to stay in the areas around Georgia and remain true to their culture instead of migrating west. They would simply adopt an outwardly European style while preserving the most important aspects of Cherokee culture.

Sequoyah was one of the Cherokee fighters who defended the United States against the British in the War of 1812. In the Battle of Horseshoe Bend, he fought under Andrew Jackson, the man who would become president and force the removal of the Cherokee people. Later, Sequoyah became a leader and fervent supporter of Cherokee sovereignty in the face of the removal effort.

Cherokee Alphabet.

Ꭰ a	Ꭱ e	Ꭲ i	Ꭳ o	Ꭴ u	Ꭵ v
Ꭶ ga Ꭷ ka	Ꭸ ge	Ꭹ gi	Ꭺ go	Ꭻ gu	Ꭼ gv
Ꭽ ha	Ꭾ he	Ꭿ hi	Ꮀ ho	Ꮁ hu	Ꮂ hv
Ꮃ la	Ꮄ le	Ꮅ li	Ꮆ lo	Ꮇ lu	Ꮈ lv
Ꮉ ma	Ꮊ me	Ꮋ mi	Ꮌ mo	Ꮍ mu	
Ꮎ na Ꮏ hna Ꮐ nah	Ꮑ ne	Ꮒ ni	Ꮓ no	Ꮔ nu	Ꮕ nv
Ꮖ qua	Ꮗ que	Ꮘ qui	Ꮙ quo	Ꮚ quu	Ꮛ quv
Ꮜ sa Ꮝ s	Ꮞ se	Ꮟ si	Ꮠ so	Ꮡ su	Ꮢ sv
Ꮣ da Ꮤ ta	Ꮥ de Ꮦ te	Ꮧ di Ꮨ ti	Ꮩ do	Ꮪ du	Ꮫ dv
Ꮬ dla Ꮭ tla	Ꮮ tle	Ꮯ tli	Ꮰ tlo	Ꮱ tlu	Ꮲ tlv
Ꮳ tsa	Ꮴ tse	Ꮵ tsi	Ꮶ tso	Ꮷ tsu	Ꮸ tsv
Ꮹ wa	Ꮺ we	Ꮻ wi	Ꮼ wo	Ꮽ wu	Ꮾ wv
Ꮿ ya	Ᏸ ye	Ᏹ yi	Ᏺ yo	Ᏻ yu	Ᏼ yv

Sounds represented by Vowels

a, as a in father, or short as a in rival
e, as a in hate, or short as e in met
i, as i in pique, or short as i in pit
o, as aw in law, or short as o in not.
u, as oo in fool, or short as u in pull.
v, as u in but, nasalized.

Consonant Sounds

g nearly as in English, but approaching to k. d nearly as in English but approaching to t. h.k.l.m.n.q.s.t.w.y. as in English. Syllables beginning with g. except Ꭶ have sometimes the power of k. Ꭺ.Ꮝ.Ꮾ. are sometimes sounded to, tu, tv: and Syllables written with tl except Ꮭ sometimes vary to dl.

The syllabary Sequoyah devised and presented to the National Council empowered Cherokees to read and write in their own language.

CHEROKEE PHOENIX.

There were many positive consequences of having their own formal language. The Cherokees were able to adopt a written constitution, establish a Supreme Court, and publish this newspaper, the Cherokee Phoenix.

As editor of the Cherokee Phoenix, *Elias Boudinot often defended the Cherokee Nation with editorials against Indian Removal.*

Another one of the men who fought for General Andrew Jackson in the War of 1812 was John Ross who, as Principal Chief, later encouraged the Cherokees to resist removal through the courts. Then, along the Trail of Tears, Chief Ross took responsibility for the health and welfare of the thousands of Cherokees who suffered through horrid conditions.

Major Ridge, the third of the major Cherokee leaders to have served at Horseshoe Bend, at first defended the Cherokee Nation's right to remain in the Southeast. He even participated in the execution of Chief Doublehead, killed because he had leased land to white settlers.

The tragedy of this infamous time in American history deepened when Major Ridge, Boudinot, and a handful of other influential Cherokees concluded further resistance was futile and agreed to removal by illegally signing the Treaty of New Echota. Thus began the Trail of Tears. At least four thousand Cherokees, nearly a quarter of their nation, died during the forced journey to the West.

John Ross, Principal Chief of the New Cherokee Nation, convened the council at Tahlequah, Oklahoma, where the Cherokees finally settled. Seventeen tribes sent delegates, and Tahlequah became a place of commerce and culture.

Mission schools (above) that originated in North Carolina were deemed necessary to the New Cherokee Nation. So that education would continue to be an integral part of Cherokee life, these schools were re-established in their new community in the West. In the rebuilding of the Cherokee Nation, Reverend Jesse Bushyhead (below) put up the first church with materials that made the treacherous journey all the way from Georgia. That church still stands.

In beloved memory of Wotkogee/Louis Littlecoon Oliver and Gogisgi/Carroll Arnett, two elders whose teachings touched so many hearts.

ACKNOWLEDGMENTS

Although I began writing this book in 1998, this story is really the result of many years of learning about Cherokee history and culture. It is impossible for me to fully acknowledge the generosity that has been shown to me over the past four decades by so many Cherokee people whose words and work have helped me better understand the many meanings of "the Trail Where the People Cried."

I owe a particular debt of gratitude to my Cherokee friends Gayle Ross, Robert and Evelyn Conley, Tom Belt, Murv Jacob, Rayna Green, and Geary Hobson. Not only have they read my work and helped me correct my mistakes (on this and other projects), they have always reminded me that Cherokee history neither begins nor ends with the Trail. And then there is my late friend Carroll Arnett, whose poems and stories first led me to start walking the Trail. Brother, I remember the paths we walked and the day we stood together to place flowers on the grave of John Ross. We miss you.

I also need to express my gratitude to the National Geographic Society for commissioning me to write a book about the Trail of Tears of the Cherokees and the Long Walk of the Navajos. The travel and research I did for that book, *Trail of Tears, Paths of Beauty,* helped prepare me for this project.

In terms of scholarship, my entry into the study of Cherokee history was the work of James Mooney. His two volumes, *The Sacred Formulas of the Cherokees* (1891) and *Myths of the Cherokee* (1900), are still vital and important. In many ways, in the care and respect he showed with the Cherokees and other native Nations, Mooney transcended his era. But, good as Mooney was for his time, his work is only a point of departure. Today, anyone interested in the history and culture of the Cherokee owes a deep debt of gratitude to the work being done by modern Cherokee scholars. Here again, there are far too many people for me to name them all, but I have to mention the incredible work of Duane H. King and Rennard Strickland and the marvelous *Journal of Cherokee Studies* published by the Museum of the Cherokee Indian in cooperation with the Cherokee Historical Association. All that I can say is that I am continuing to read and to listen and I am in awe of their brilliance and devotion. And I wholeheartedly agree with Rennard Strickland that when you get to know the Cherokees, you cannot help but love them.

More than anyone else, though, I have to thank Louis Littlecoon Oliver, a Creek Indian elder whose deep knowledge of the Muskogee, Yuchi, and Cherokee cultures was only matched by his humility and his gentle sense of humor. I will never forget the times we spent together in Tahlequah. It was Grandfather Louis who placed a Cherokee Rose in my hand and then burned cedar for me on the mountaintop. Wado, wado.

Grateful acknowledgment is made for permission to reprint the following:

Cover Portrait: Detail from a James Mooney photograph of a group of stick-ball players, courtesy of the Smithsonian Institution/National Anthropological Archives.

Cover background: *Trail of Tears* by Robert Lindneux, courtesy of SuperStock.

Foldout map illustration by Bryn Barnard.

Page 188 (top): Photograph of stick-ball players by James Mooney, courtesy of the Smithsonian Institution/National Anthropological Archives.

Page 188 (bottom): Lithograph of Cherokees, ©Collection of the New-York Historical Society.

Page 189: Sequoyah, courtesy of the Archives & Manuscripts Division of the Oklahoma Historical Society.

Page 190: Cherokee syllabary, courtesy of the Smithsonian Institution/National Anthropological Archives.

Page 191 (top): *Cherokee Phoenix*, courtesy of the Library of Congress.

Page 191 (bottom): Elias Boudinot, courtesy of the Archives & Manuscripts Division of the Oklahoma Historical Society.

Page 192: Detail of Cherokee Chief John Ross, courtesy of the Archives & Manuscripts Division of the Oklahoma Historical Society.

Page 193: Major Ridge, courtesy of the Smithsonian Institution/National Anthropological Archives.

Page 194 (top): *Trail of Tears* by Robert Lindneux, courtesy of SuperStock.

Page 194 (bottom): Meeting of Council at Tahlequah, courtesy of the Smithsonian Institution/National Anthropological Archives.

Page 195 (top): Mission School, courtesy of the Smithsonian Institution/National Anthropological Archives.

Page 195 (bottom): Reverend Bushyhead, courtesy of the Archives & Manuscripts Division of the Oklahoma Historical Society.

About the Author

Of writing *The Journal of Jesse Smoke,* Joseph Bruchac says, "One of the heroes of my childhood was Sequoyah, the Cherokee man whose syllabary enabled the Cherokees to write their own langauge in a truly Indian way. I cannot remember a time when I was not fascinated by the history and the stories of those who call themselves Ani-yanega, the Principal People. Part of it, I suppose, is my own American Indian ancestry. However, my Indian blood is Abenaki, a Native nation far to the north of the Cherokees. Though our people have many things in common with the Cherokees, including being driven from much of our original homeland, to do justice to this story I had to spend years in the process of learning with the help of many Cherokee people. That kind of learning teaches you patience. I would not have been able to write this story twenty years ago, even though I thought of doing such a novel more than once. I am glad that I waited.

"More than virtually any other Native nation, the Cherokee have long been writing and publishing their own stories, both in Sequoyah's syllabary and in English. A number of journals that actually were kept by Cherokees on the Trail of Tears are in collections, and I have been told that even more such journals are kept in the possession of Cherokee families whose ancestors were on the Trail. Reading what was written along the Trail by Cherokees and some of the white people who accompanied them meant even more to me, though, when I walked the Trail myself. I began at the place called Kituwa, an ancient mound in North Carolina where many Cherokees say their people first came into the world. Later that day, standing on top of Clingman's Dome, a tall mountain sacred to the Cherokees, my friend Tom Belt, a Cherokee language teacher, pointed out to me the route the trail followed and the places in the valleys below where the stockades were built to hold the Cherokees after they were rounded up by the army. I am not ashamed to say that tears came to my eyes more than once that day.

"If there is anything in this journal that is moving or memorable, that strength comes from the Cherokee people. I am grateful for the generosity they have always shown me. If there are any mistakes, they are my own and I apologize for them. I am only one small voice between Earth and Sky. Like the Cherokees, Earth and Sky will be here long after I am gone."

Joseph Bruchac is the author of numerous books for children, many of which concern Cherokee history and culture. His many honors and awards include the American Book Award for *Breaking Silence;* the 1986 Cherokee Nation Prose Award; and Yaddo Residency Fellowships in 1984 and 1985. Recently, his book *The Heart of a Chief* was named a 1999 Jane Addams Children's Book Award Honor Book. Mr. Bruchac lives with his wife in Greenfield Center, New York.

Other books in the My Name Is America series

The Journal of William Thomas Emerson
A Revolutionary War Patriot
by Barry Denenberg

The Journal of James Edmond Pease
A Civil War Union Soldier
by Jim Murphy

The Journal of Joshua Loper
A Black Cowboy
by Walter Dean Myers

The Journal of Scott Pendleton Collins
A World War II Soldier
by Walter Dean Myers

The Journal of Sean Sullivan
A Transcontinental Railroad Worker
by William Durbin

The Journal of Ben Uchida
Citizen 13559, Mirror Lake Internment Camp
by Barry Denenberg

The Journal of Jasper Jonathan Pierce
A Pilgrim Boy
by Ann Rinaldi

The Journal of Wong Ming-Chung
A Chinese Miner
by Laurence Yep

The Journal of Augustus Pelletier
The Lewis and Clark Expedition
by Kathryn Lasky

The Journal of Otto Peltonen
A Finnish Immigrant
by William Durbin

The Journal of Biddy Owens
The Negro Leagues
by Walter Dean Myers

While the events described and some of the characters in this book may be based on actual historical events and real people, Jesse Smoke is a fictional character, created by the author, and his journal and its epilogue are works of fiction.

Library of Congress Cataloging-in-Publication Data

Bruchac, Joseph, 1942–
The journal of Jesse Smoke : a Cherokee boy / by Joseph Bruchac.
p. cm. — (My name is America)
Summary: Jesse Smoke, a sixteen-year-old Cherokee, begins a journal in 1837 to record stories of his people and their difficulties as they face removal along the Trail of Tears. Includes a historical note giving details of the removal.
ISBN 0-439-12197-3
1. Trail of Tears, 1838 — Juvenile fiction. 2. Cherokee Indians — History — Juvenile fiction. [1. Trail of Tears, 1838 — Fiction. 2. Cherokee Indians — History — Fiction. 3. Indians of North America — Southern states — History — Fiction. 4. Diaries — Ficiton.] I. Title. II. Series.

PZ7.B82816 Jo 2001
[FIC] — dc21 00-055619

10 9 8 7 6 5 4 3 2 1 01 02 03 04 05

The display type was set in Trackpad.
The text type was set in Berling.
Book design by Elizabeth B. Parisi
Photo research by Zoe Moffitt

Printed in the U.S.A
First printing, June 2001